DEADLY PAST

VERONA BAY

Katie Reus

Cover art: Jaycee of Sweet 'N Spicy Designs
Editor: Kelli Collins
Author website: https://www.katiereus.com

Publisher's Note: This is a work of fiction. Names, characters, places, and incidents are either the products of the author's imagination or used fictitiously, and any resemblance to actual persons, living or dead, or business establishments, organizations or locales is completely coincidental.

Deadly Past /Katie Reus. -- 1st ed.
KR Press, LLC

ISBN-13: 9781635561432

For all the dreamers, creators, and artists out there! Keep doing what you're doing. You're all changing the world one day at a time with your art (whatever medium that may be). Now more than ever, we need art and entertainment.

Praise for the novels of Katie Reus

"Exciting in more ways than one, well-paced and smoothly written, I'd recommend *A Covert Affair* to any romantic suspense reader."
—Harlequin Junkie

"Sexy military romantic suspense." —USA Today

"I could not put this book down. . . . Let me be clear that I am not saying that this was a good book *for* a paranormal genre; it was an excellent romance read, *period*." —All About Romance

"Reus strikes just the right balance of steamy sexual tension and nail-biting action....This romantic thriller reliably hits every note that fans of the genre will expect." —*Publishers Weekly*

"Prepare yourself for the start of a great new series! . . . I'm excited about reading more about this great group of characters."
—Fresh Fiction

"Wow! This powerful, passionate hero sizzles with sheer deliciousness. I loved every sexy twist of this fun & exhilarating tale. Katie Reus delivers!" —Carolyn Crane, RITA award winning author

"A sexy, well-crafted paranormal romance that succeeds with smart characters and creative world building."—Kirkus Reviews

"*Mating Instinct*'s romance is taut and passionate . . . Katie Reus's newest installment in her Moon Shifter series will leave readers breathless!"
—Stephanie Tyler, *New York Times* bestselling author

"You'll fall in love with Katie's heroes."
—*New York Times* bestselling author, Kaylea Cross

"Both romantic and suspenseful, a fast-paced sexy book full of high stakes action." —Heroes and Heartbreakers

"Katie Reus pulls the reader into a story line of second chances, betrayal, and the truth about forgotten lives and hidden pasts."
—The Reading Café

"Nonstop action, a solid plot, good pacing, and riveting suspense."
—RT Book Reviews

"Enough sexual tension to set the pages on fire."
—*New York Times* bestselling author, Alexandra Ivy

"...a wild hot ride for readers. The story grabs you and doesn't let go."
—*New York Times* bestselling author, Cynthia Eden

"Has all the right ingredients: a hot couple, evil villains, and a killer action-filled plot. . . . [The] Moon Shifter series is what I call Grade-A entertainment!" —Joyfully Reviewed

"*Avenger's Heat* hits the ground running...This is a story of strength, of partnership and healing, and it does it brilliantly."
—Vampire Book Club

"*Mating Instinct* was a great read with complex characters, serious political issues and a world I am looking forward to coming back to."
—All Things Urban Fantasy

PROLOGUE

Ana slid the cap off her Canon camera as she approached the next alleyway. She was working on a project for her mentor and boss, highlighting poverty around the area. This was her last night, and she'd already gotten some incredible shots. It was nearing midnight, and she was almost ready to head back to the studio.

She'd been down here enough over the years—she'd spent a lot of time on these very streets because she and her mom had been homeless her freshman and sophomore years of high school. It hadn't been an easy childhood but she was a hell of a lot more comfortable down here than most of her friends from college.

At the entrance to the alleyway, she could see two men arguing, one man shoving the other up against the crumbling brick wall. Instead of using it as a shortcut, she turned back and continued along the sidewalk. She might be comfortable down here but she didn't have a death wish. Violence wasn't terrible in the area, but it happened. And if that was two addicts fighting over something, she didn't want to be anywhere near them.

The sidewalks of this particular street were in decent shape. The money center store and the pawn shop both had bars over their windows, but the barber shop and bodega didn't. She waved at Mr. Sanz, the owner of the bodega—a man she adored. When she and her mom had been living on the streets here, he'd given them what he could, one of many people to help them get on their feet.

"Ana!" He stopped sweeping and set the broom against the closed front door. "What are you doing here so late?" he asked, even as he answered his own question. "Still always taking pictures, I see."

She laughed lightly and nodded. "Of course." On impulse, she lifted her camera and snapped a picture of the front of his bodega. Then him.

He laughed in that genuine way of his that always pulled a smile from her. The man had been married for forty years, had five grown girls and was like a fixture here.

"How's business?" she asked.

He lifted a shoulder. "Still paying the bills."

She grinned at his typical answer. "Good. I hear Ale," his oldest daughter, Alejandra, "got promoted." Ana didn't know the specifics, just that it was something to do with the local District's Attorney office.

The smile he gave her could have lit up the whole street. "My girl will be running that office in a few years. We're so proud."

"As you should be."

"We're proud of you too. Hector tells me you'll be famous one day."

She snorted softly, shaking her head at the praise. Hector, her boss and mentor, was always telling people that. She was simply happy he believed in her at all. "I just hope to be able to do what I love." For her, art had always been a constant. Art and books, which were essentially the same things, just different mediums. Books and her photography had kept her sane during the tough years, taught her to see the world through a different lens. Pun intended.

He made a scoffing sound. "Nonsense, if he says it, it's true. I heard you graduated with honors. We really are proud of you. The whole neighborhood."

She swallowed hard as unexpected tears stung her eyes, but quickly blinked them away. "Thank you. I don't think I'd be here if not for the kindness of you and others. I'll forever be grateful."

Now he was the one who waved away her thanks, as if uncomfortable with it. Stepping back, he opened the door for a woman she recognized as a nurse. Must have just gotten off the late shift.

"I'll let you get back to it," she murmured. "See you soon."

Picking up his broom, he nodded and followed the woman inside. Five minutes later, Ana let herself into Hector's art studio with her key and locked herself in immediately. She wanted to expose the images from tonight, then head home and enjoy a long soak in her tub.

She hurried through the art studio, able to navigate around the displays even in the dimness. In the hallway, she headed for the dark room, but paused when she saw movement flash on one of the security feeds as she passed by Hector's office. He'd gone home hours ago but his security camera worked 24/7.

She stepped into the office and bent over the desk, scanning the feeds. It was difficult to make out what was going on but it looked like someone was dumping something into their dumpster.

She let out an annoyed grumble. It had to be the owner of the new Italian restaurant two blocks over. Over the last month, he'd been sending someone to dump all their old food here and other places on the block, instead of using his own damn dumpster. Well, not tonight.

Annoyance spiking, she hurried out of the room and stalked to the back door. She quickly undid the deadbolt and flipped on the security light—which she'd told Hector he needed to upgrade to a sensory one. Whoever this jackass was, he was about to get a big surprise.

As she stepped out into the alleyway, a man who looked to be about her age, likely still in college, was hoisting something—someone!—into the dumpster.

Oh my God. Those were bare legs. A scrap of pink. Red streaking down the woman's unmoving legs.

Ana froze, her breaths sawing in and out as her gaze connected with his.

He let go and the body tumbled into the dumpster. He stared at her, the dark depths of his eyes immediately filling with anger as he rushed toward her.

On instinct, she lifted her camera and started taking pictures with the flash. She needed to blind him, to escape. To call for help.

Flash. Flash. Flash.

He let out a growl of rage that sounded animalistic as he sprinted for her.

She turned and raced back inside, slamming the deadbolt into place right as a huge thump pounded against the door.

Bang! Bang! Bang!

He couldn't get through the steel door, she knew that, but she still sprinted away from it and raced to the office where she'd left her cell phone. Heart racing and palms damp, she called 911 immediately. Calling the cops wasn't normally her first choice but it couldn't be avoided. Not now.

"911 operator, how may I assist you?"

"I just saw someone dumping a body! I need help. I'm at Las Olas art studio off of Berger Street."

The sound of breaking glass made her freeze. Had the guy broken into the front door? She hadn't reset the alarm or anything. *Oh my God, oh my God, oh my God!*

"I think he's inside the studio," she whispered, terrified.

"Ma'am, I have backup on the way. They're seven minutes out." The operator's voice was so calm, it made Ana want to be calm too. "You need to find somewhere to hide."

Ana remained quiet as she peered out of the office doorway. This door was too flimsy to lock and hide behind. She needed to get to the dark room—with its enforced door and deadbolt. She heard a thump and then a clatter of something skittering across the floor. Whoever it was must have run into one of their displays.

Her heartbeat an erratic tattoo in her chest, she crept down the hallway toward where the security panel was. The cops might be on their way but something told her the only thing that might scare this person away was setting off an actual alarm. As she reached the panel, she pressed the only red button.

Immediately the siren pierced the air, and she quickly ducked into the dark room, locking the door behind her. It wasn't steel, but she could at least try to hide. Flipping off the dim red light, she crossed the pitch-dark room from memory.

"Ma'am?"

"I can't talk now," she whispered to the operator. She heard the woman say something but didn't respond. She couldn't make her voice work anymore, not when fear was clogging her throat.

She hurried to a closet and ducked inside, pulling the door closed behind her. Then she tucked her phone into her jeans pocket and silently prayed. She hadn't prayed since she was fourteen, but right now she figured it might help.

She wasn't sure how much time passed but it felt like an eternity as she remained in that small closet. The familiar scent of acetic acid overpowered most of the other scents, giving her an odd sense of comfort.

The alarm abruptly stopped and she jolted against the door at the shock to her senses.

She blinked into the darkness and the sudden quiet, then jumped at the sound of pounding on the dark room door.

With trembling fingers, she pulled her cell phone out of her pocket. Without the blare of the alarm, she could hear again, and it looked like the operator was still on the phone.

"Police!" A commanding male voice called from somewhere outside.

"Someone saying they're the police are here," she whispered into her cell. "I'm hiding in the dark room."

"They've secured the studio," the operator said. "You're safe now. I'm going to let them know you're going to come out. Okay?"

She shoved out a breath. "Okay."

Unable to stop trembling, she opened the closet and braced for an attack, even though she knew it was unlikely. She reached along the wall and stopped when she felt a switch, then turned it on. A soft amber glow lit up the room, giving her eyes time to adjust. There was no one there. "I'm coming out right now," she told the operator.

Time seemed to slow as she walked across the small dark room, everything about tonight taking on a surreal quality. She opened the door to find one man and one woman both in uniform.

"Ana Diaz?" the woman asked.

She stared, wondering how the woman knew her name. Had she told the operator? She didn't think so.

"You called using your cell phone?" the woman continued. "That's the name that showed up on caller ID."

Oh, right. She nodded, her throat sticking for a moment. "I did. And yes, I'm Ana." She cleared her throat, forcing herself to talk. "I saw someone on our security camera. A man. He was… he had a body in his arms. Did you guys find him? He broke in here."

"No." The two shared a glance, then looked back at her. The woman continued, apparently the spokesperson for the duo. "But we did find a body in the dumpster out back. We're going to need to talk to you about everything you saw. You'll need to make an official statement."

She nodded, a shudder wracking her shoulders. The last time she'd talked to the police was when she'd found her mom's body. "Of course. I took pictures of the guy with my camera," she said, motioning to the Canon around her neck. "I can develop them for you if you need." She didn't want them taking her camera for evidence, but they could have the film. And a picture of the guy dumping the body would be a hell of a lot better than a description from her—though she could easily sketch his face from memory. It was embedded into her brain.

Both officers' eyes widened slightly even as they nodded simultaneously, as if they'd choreographed it. Their surprise was clear, but they liked what she had to say.

"You can do it now?" asked the woman with dark hair pulled into a tight bun—whose nametag read Officer Ramos.

"Yes. It'll take forty minutes, give or take."

She quickly spoke into her radio, then turned back to Ana and nodded again. "Do what you need to do. Then you can make your statement. If we have a picture, we'll be able to find this guy a hell of a lot faster."

"I need to call Hector, my boss. He owns this place."

"He's already out front. He was alerted when the alarm went off."

Relief slid through her, knowing that he was here. He must have been the one to turn off the security system. "I'm going to lock the dark room so no one accidentally comes in while I'm developing the film. Okay?"

Officer Ramos nodded. "I'll stand guard anyway. No one will come in or out."

Ana simply stepped back into the room, her fingers trembling as she got to work. There really had been a body in the dumpster. She'd seen a man dumping a woman's body—and she'd gotten his face on camera.

CHAPTER ONE

Ten years later

Autumn hurried through the front door of Verona Bay's local bank five minutes before it was about to close. She normally didn't come inside but the ATM wasn't working and she wanted to deposit a few checks. She needed a new deck and was saving up to put in a pool for next summer. Doing any of that on a teacher's salary was always a stretch, so any extra money she got from her art classes or commissioned projects, she socked away.

"Autumn, how are you?" Melissa Weprin, the manager of the bank, asked with a smile as she stepped outside of her glass-windowed office.

"Hey, Melissa. Just depositing some checks before the weekend. What's up with the ATM?"

"Oh, it's got to be serviced. So will I see you at Bianca's pool party tomorrow?"

"You know I wouldn't miss it." School started next week, and she planned to enjoy every last moment of her summer. She loved what she did, loved teaching kids about art and seeing the amazing things they came up with.

Ten years ago, the thought of teaching would have made her roll her eyes, but life had a way of shaking everything up. She knew firsthand.

So while she wasn't doing what she'd once dreamed of, she'd still made an amazing life. And she'd made the choice a long time ago not to feel sorry for herself—even if there were some dreams she'd had to bury.

"I hope you bring that sangria," Melissa said, laughing as she headed for the front door, presumably to lock it, given the time.

"It wouldn't be a party without it." Laughing lightly, she stepped away and got in the short line.

She glanced over her shoulder at the sound of a commotion—then froze as two men wearing masks and carrying huge guns kicked the door open, sending Melissa sprawling onto the tile floor.

Autumn stared in horror as one of them locked the door and turned to face everyone, gun raised.

"Everybody on the ground!" the taller of the two men shouted.

They both had on the creepy white masks from the movie Scream, making them look terrifying.

Autumn didn't pause at their order, she hit the ground and covered her head. But she turned her head sideways and peeked over her arm, watching the men jump into action.

She'd seen reports about bank robbers on the news. This crew of two men had been robbing banks along the East Coast of Florida for the last couple weeks. She'd never imagined they would target Verona Bay. Which was stupid as hell, because no place was safe. She knew that more than most.

She watched booted feet stomp across the tile toward the glass-encased tellers. So far these guys hadn't killed anybody, and she hoped they would just take what they wanted and leave as they'd done at other banks.

"Open the second door or I start blowing off heads," the tall one shouted as he held a gun up to what was likely bullet-resistant glass.

Blood rushed in her ears as she watched Gloria, the woman behind the glass, stare at him, crying.

"I've got the key to the door and the safe," Melissa said, making Autumn whip her head around even though she was trying to remain as still as possible.

The other man had a gun trained on Melissa as she approached, cool, calm and collected, with the keys jingling in her hands.

Heart racing, Autumn watched as her friend hurried to the door and opened it. One of the men rushed through it and started shouting at the teller to empty the drawers. Thankfully, Gloria managed to jerk out of her shock and start following orders.

Just do what they say, Autumn mentally shouted at her. She didn't want anyone hurt... or worse.

"I know you've got more cash in the back," the other man snapped at Melissa.

She nodded and turned toward the door that would lead to the vault. Then Melissa and the man ducked out of sight for a long sixty seconds.

Despite the air-conditioned building, sweat rolled down Autumn's back, pooling at the base of her spine. She slowly, carefully glanced around, took in all of the bank. There was no security guard visible. But the cameras were recording everything. She recognized a man who worked for the local hardware store on the floor near the bathroom door, and her eyes widened in surprise when she saw a teacher she worked with crouching on the ground on the other side of the bank. The woman was half in, half out of one of the offices. She must've been in a meeting and dropped where she stood when the men infiltrated the bank.

There were a few others she recognized, all with their faces buried in their arms as they remained immobile on the ground.

Moments later, Melissa stepped out, her hands trembling slightly as the bank robber clutched a blue duffel bag over his shoulder. His gun was pointed at the ground at least. "I got it," he snapped out. "Let's go!"

The man with the teller grabbed his own bag and leaned close to Gloria. "Good, this bitch is too slow," he snarled before turning away from her and stalking out.

A cacophony of noise blasted the air as the tall man started shooting at the ceiling, sending plaster flying everywhere. *Bang. Bang. Bang.*

A scream caught in Autumn's throat as part of the ceiling landed in a heap two feet in front of her, but she didn't let it escape. Tensing, she covered her head, all her muscles taut even when it suddenly went deathly quiet.

The men sprinted for the doors, throwing them open before racing out.

Melissa hurried after them, her heels clicking wildly. She immediately locked the doors even as Autumn grabbed for her purse and pulled out her cell phone. She didn't think, she simply called her neighbor—Sheriff Lincoln Jordan. She didn't call 911, but his personal cell phone. Later she might think about why that was, when she'd taken to avoiding him in general.

But she knew without a doubt that he would be here if she called.

"Autumn, hey," he said after the first ring.

"I'm at the bank. It was just robbed by two armed men," she rasped out, her voice thready. "They had on masks but I think it's the guys robbing banks up the coast. The ones from the news. They literally just ran out."

He softly cursed. "Are you okay?"

"I'm fine." Not true, but it didn't matter. She was alive and *that* was what mattered.

"Okay. I'll be there in two minutes. Hang tight." He hung up, and she finally shoved to her feet. "Lincoln's on his way," she said to Melissa, who had her own cell phone out.

Her friend nodded, her expression tense even as she spoke to the 911 operator.

Looking around, Autumn saw that Mrs. Ackerley was quietly crying in the corner. She hurried over to her and checked to make sure she hadn't been injured by a ricochet bullet.

In the distance, she heard sirens, and the sound brought up a whole lot of bad memories but she squashed them fast, locking them up tight.

"You're okay," she said as she gently held the older woman's trembling hands. "We're all okay."

Mrs. Ackerley blinked and shook her head as her tears dried up. She looked as if she was coming out of a fog. "This weekend is my granddaughter's first birthday. I thought... I thought we were all going to die."

Autumn pulled her into a hug and was surprised by the woman's tight grip as she hugged her back.

The door flung open again, and her body tensed as she turned at the sound of the little bell.

But raw relief punched through her the moment she made eye contact with Lincoln. His green eyes immediately sought her out—pinned her in place with a long stare before sweeping over her. The look was purely clinical, but the tightness in his shoulders lessened the smallest bit when he saw she was okay.

Then he turned to Melissa, all business as he started talking to her.

Autumn... didn't know what to do with that look from him. That *concern*. She didn't know what to do about her attraction to him in general. She'd been ignoring it for months. Ignoring him as best she could, even if he was her neighbor.

And that was what she would continue to do.

CHAPTER TWO

Lincoln rubbed a hand over his damp hair, exhausted from the evening's events as he looked out the side window toward his neighbor's house. Autumn Perez, his very sexy, remote neighbor he wanted to get to know a hell of a lot more.

He could see a few lights on so he knew she was still awake. It was only nine, but she'd been stuck talking to the Feds and his own people for a couple hours after they'd secured the bank.

He'd been there even after she'd left, talking to the team of Feds who were hunting the bank robbers along the East Coast, taking statements, making sure everyone got home safely and talking to the media. At this point, he was beyond exhausted.

But he wouldn't be able to sleep until he'd seen for himself that Autumn would be okay tonight. They'd talked at the bank but it had been a rush of people and noise, and he was feeling protective of her.

It had been like that since she'd moved in next door to him a year ago, and he wasn't sure why.

That was a lie. He found her insanely attractive.

She was petite, maybe five feet two inches, with long, thick dark hair she normally wore in a ponytail. Her dark brown eyes had flecks of amber in them if the light hit them right. And she always had paint spots or ink on her fingernails or on her hands. She also had another kind of ink covering her arms—tattoos he wanted to see more of.

She was the local art teacher at the high school and did a lot of extra classes around town. And the more he found out about her, the more he liked her. He'd discovered that she was good friends with Serenity, his soon-to-be sister-in-law, a woman he'd known since college and adored. A woman who'd been through hell.

Sighing at himself, he trekked next door and knocked softly. If she didn't answer, he would head back home. He never wanted her to feel like he was trying to invade her personal space, and it was clear that she liked hers. She'd put up very clear boundaries with him, refusing to even call him by name. It was always "Sheriff", not Lincoln.

She opened the door a few moments later and a whisper of surprise flickered across her face before she gave him a real smile. An honest to God *smile* that changed her entire countenance and made her look a decade younger, as if she were fresh out of college.

"Lincoln, hey. Is everything okay?" Her dark eyes were warm tonight as she watched him.

She really must be feeling out of sorts to call him by his first name. "Yeah. I just… Honestly, I just wanted to check on you. Today was a lot for anyone, and you held up at the bank like a boss." Both she and Melissa had, handling everything with a certain sort of fortitude that had been impressive.

She gave him another, smaller smile as she stepped back. "I'm doing all right. And I was about to pour myself some wine. You want some?"

He didn't actually drink wine but no way in hell was he saying no to spending time with Autumn. He'd convert to being a wine drinker if that was what it took.

"Thanks." As he stepped inside, a black and white Border Collie peeked around the corner of a club chair by the window. Her little head tilted slightly to the side as she cautiously watched him.

His eyebrows raised in surprise. "I didn't know you had a dog." Normally dogs ran to see who was at a front door, but it was clear this one was skittish.

She snorted. "I just got her about a month ago. Her name's Shadow and she's a rescue. I swear she's more like a cat than a dog. Instead of running for the door when anyone stops by, she hides. Just give her time, she'll warm up to you in a minute."

He half-waved at the dog then felt kind of foolish, but when he saw the smile on Autumn's face, he thought maybe not so foolish after all. He was definitely a dog person and had been planning on getting one in the next year as well—if his schedule ever cleared up.

Inside the kitchen, he took in everything with interest. She'd made a lot of changes from the previous owner. He'd known she'd had construction done here before she moved in. There'd been a whole crew of people ripping out the old carpet, putting in new floors and doing other things before he'd even met her. But seeing all the changes were incredible.

"You really have an eye for design," he said as he took in the mix of modern and eclectic. The walls were a pale gray, the floors a dark wood, and there were pops of color everywhere, from the art to the throw blankets and pillows. "And those photographs are incredible." They were pictures of downtown Verona Bay, some of the outlying areas, and various shots from different festivals. Six had been blown up and they covered one of her kitchen walls. The images were... striking. "Where did you get them?"

When he looked back at her, her cheeks were flushed pink. "Thanks, I actually took them."

"I didn't know you were into photography. I knew you painted but apparently you're multitalented."

She made a scoffing sound as she pulled down two glasses. When she did, the sleeve of the oversized sweater she wore fell back, revealing one of her tattoos— a cluster of dainty-looking white flowers winding up her inner arm. "I like to dabble in all sorts of mediums. I find that it keeps things fresh." She saw him looking and half-smiled. "You like my ink?"

"I do. What's the meaning behind that one?" Because something told him that she wouldn't get tattoos that didn't mean something.

She shoved up her sleeve and held it as she stretched out her arm. "Ah, this one is Lily of the Valley flowers. I got it for a couple reasons—they were my mom's favorite and even though they're delicate, they're tough. They survive harsh winters and always bloom in the spring.

Plus, they're poisonous, so animals give them a wide berth."

"I like it." And he liked her. He motioned toward her wall of art as she let her sleeve drop. "You could sell some of those pictures." They had enough festivals, farmers markets and hell, even the local art gallery would display her work. He might not know much about art, but he knew that those were professional-quality pictures that people would want.

She simply shrugged and poured both of them a glass of red. "For some reason I don't think you're actually a wine guy, so if you don't want this you won't hurt my feelings."

He grinned as he sat down at the island countertop. "I prefer beer but my mom has gotten me to try a few of the bottles she got on her last trip to Italy."

"Your mom is one of a kind," Autumn said as she sat down across from him. Her fingernails were a bright coral color and, sure enough, random flecks of colors dotted her fingers.

"I didn't know that you knew her."

"Pretty sure everyone knows Mrs. Jordan, mom of the three hellions from Verona Bay." Her full lips quirked up slightly before she took a sip of her wine.

"We weren't hellions." And she wouldn't know because she hadn't been raised here, had only moved here recently.

"So the rumors *aren't* true?"

Now he grinned. "Only some of them."

Laughter in her dark eyes, she took another sip of her wine, sighing in appreciation. The black and white sweater she wore hung slightly off her shoulder, revealing smooth bronze skin he wanted to kiss.

Something he didn't need to be thinking about. "So how are you feeling, honestly?"

She paused, as if weighing her answer. "Shaken up. Everything happened so fast. They rushed in, shouted orders, and just... took what they wanted with violence. It was like a surreal dream, like it was happening to someone else." She shuddered then and wrapped her arms around herself as she looked him in the eye.

"I'm glad no one was hurt. The Feds will catch those guys."

"I hope so. They could have hurt someone. Killed any of us with a ricochet bullet."

He paused for a moment, debating on how much he should tell her. "Between us, the Feds are already closing in on them anyway, but they managed to figure out who the buyer of the bullets was from some of the casings. It confirmed what they suspected." They had the names of the robbers but weren't releasing it to the public yet.

She raised her eyebrows at that, took another sip of her wine. "Well then I guess I'm glad they made a stupid mistake. It was all so... unnecessarily violent." She shook her head and set down her glass. "I sometimes wonder what goes wrong with some people, how their lives might've turned out differently if they'd made different choices." She glanced at her wall of pictures... and for a moment he didn't even think she was aware of him. But then she shook her head and looked back at him, giving him a smile. "You were really good with everyone today," she said, surprising him.

"It's my job."

"It might be your job, but I've seen the way some cops handle things. You made everyone feel safe even with all the Feds milling about. They were actually pretty decent too." She seemed surprised by that, something he mentally noted.

He nodded because he knew the team of agents working the case. He didn't know what to say and felt unnerved by her praise, as well as by the intense stare she was giving him. Thankfully at that moment, Shadow trotted in and started sniffing his feet and ankles, so he remained very still.

He smiled down at the dog and held out his hand. Shadow deigned to sniff it and must have decided she trusted him because she jumped up, planting her paws on his knee and begging for affection. Laughing, he started scratching behind her ear and bent down so she could lick his face to death.

Autumn grinned as he sat back up, which made it completely worth it. "Apparently you have a fan. She must really like you."

"I still can't believe you have dog I didn't know about. Does she even bark?"

She shook her head. "Nope. Not even when I take her for walks in the evening and let her run in the backyard, but she is definitely a homebody. She loves being with me. I'm a little worried about leaving her when school starts, but my hours are fairly decent so she shouldn't be home by herself too long. I actually might hire a service to come walk her while I'm gone, just so she gets extra interaction. She really is like a cat though, she even curls up by my head at night."

At that thought, his mind immediately went to her bed, what it looked like, what *she* would look like stretched out in it. He'd had too many fantasies about what Autumn would look like naked, stretched out under him as he brought her pleasure. But he shut that down fast and hard. He was just here as a *neighbor*.

Only a neighbor, he repeated to himself.

Shadow, who he was still petting, finally jumped off his knees and raced for her food bowl.

Lincoln stood then, not wanting to overstay his welcome.

Autumn set her wine glass down too and rounded the island. "Thank you for stopping by, seriously. I really appreciate it, Lincoln."

He wasn't sure if it was the fact that she'd said his name again, but simply hearing his name on her lips sent a jolt of... something through him. He knew what it was, even if he didn't want to define it. Without thought, his gaze dipped to her full, kissable lips.

And that was when he realized she was trembling. Oh hell. "Autumn?"

She wrapped her arms around herself. "I don't know what's wrong with me. I'm so damn cold right now. I thought I was handling everything okay, but I keep seeing everything replay in slow motion. I mean... I should be *fine*. I've dealt with worse." She snapped her mouth shut and wrapped her arms tighter around herself at that.

He filed away *that* knowledge for later. But he also didn't pressure her for more information. Her private life was her private life and she was a law-abiding citizen, as far as he knew. He wouldn't break her privacy and dig into her past.

On instinct, he reached out and gently set his hands on her shoulders. "They're gone, far from town. If they follow on the same trajectory, they'll be hours north of us and into Georgia by tomorrow. Unless the Feds catch them, which I'm hopeful they will."

To his surprise, she took a small step forward, and he wasn't sure how it happened, but suddenly she had her arms wrapped around him. He didn't hold back either, just held her tight as her trembling finally stopped.

"Normally I'm not such a mess," she murmured against his chest. A subtle citrusy scent teased his nose, something all Autumn. "And you are a very good neighbor."

He laughed lightly as she pulled back to look up at him.

For a hot moment, her gaze landed on his mouth and he saw raw, burning desire there. It sparked hot, a wild flash of fire, and he moved without thinking, dipping his head to hers.

He told himself to stop, that they were neighbors and this was definitely a mistake, but she clutched onto his shirt and tugged him down the rest of the way.

That was the thing that spurred him into action. She reached for him. Autumn actually reached—*for him.*

The second their mouths touched, it was like an incendiary reaction. He swore sparks exploded as he hoisted her up onto the island countertop.

He teased his tongue against hers as she practically devoured him, energy humming through her body, an electric live wire. When she tugged at his shirt, he didn't even think, just ripped it over his head. He was vaguely aware of the dog running from the room, but all his focus was on Autumn.

The way she tasted, the way she gently bit his bottom lip, the soft little sigh she made as he pulled her sweater over her head.

And when he saw that she wasn't wearing a bra, he groaned. Her nipples were a light brown, her breasts small, perfect and just a handful. More than enough for him. She was perfection—and he wasn't walking away from this chance with her.

He just hoped this was more than a one-time thing.

CHAPTER THREE

Autumn drank her coffee, barely tasting it. Which was just disappointing since she looked forward to coffee every morning. Last night had been... She did *not* want to call it a mistake. It hadn't been one, exactly, but it had definitely been a poorly thought-out choice.

One she'd made four times over the course of the night.

Lincoln had been a machine. A very sexy one with skilled hands and a wicked mouth. And she'd been so damn touch starved for ages. Not that she could put it all on that—she'd wanted *Lincoln*. Had ever since she'd met the straight-laced sheriff. God, what was wrong with her?

She'd actually slept with her neighbor. Though there hadn't been much sleeping involved.

She silently groaned and took another sip of her coffee as she looked out over her backyard. Shadow was outside running around, chasing a butterfly and completely entertaining herself right now. Her pink and red roses were blooming, not that she did much to curate them, they were wild and grew when they felt like it. The pops of color against the lush greenery were vivid.

"Something smells good." The rumble of Lincoln's dark, delicious voice wrapped around her as she turned to face him.

Oh God. How was he even sexier in the light of day? He strode into the kitchen with no shirt on looking half awake, his dark hair mussed, which just made him look even more rugged. He looked so delectable in just boxer briefs, and that fine, powerful body that had brought her so much pleasure last night.

"Morning," she murmured, her gaze roaming over his hard pecs and six pack. "There's a full pot of coffee."

He more or less stumbled to the pot which, yep, was adorable.

She bit back a groan. Why had she ever slept with him? She'd kept him at arm's length since moving in, but last night, something inside her had shifted. She'd simply needed to touch someone, needed sex, needed to feel alive. But she wouldn't have reached for just anyone. Nope. Apparently she had a type—*Lincoln.*

Not that it mattered. She would be putting them back into the box they'd been in before. The one labeled friendship. This had been a one-time thing. Actually saying the words out loud, however, was going to be difficult—and awkward.

She cleared her throat. "Look, last night was amazing." Though that verb didn't remotely cover her feelings. She didn't think there were enough descriptive words to explain how wonderful last night had been. She was sore in places she couldn't remember being sore before. Probably because she hadn't had sex in forever.

He turned to face her, his incredible six pack on display—and his expression was dry. "Why do I think I'm not going to like what you say next?" He took a sip of his coffee, watching her carefully over the rim of the mug that said "number one art teacher".

She cleared her throat again. "We're neighbors. If we jump into something, it has the possibility to end *really* badly. I'm certainly not moving, and I doubt you are either. I think we should call last night what it was and be done with it."

"So what was last night?" His voice was carefully neutral as he continued to watch her with those stunning eyes.

She'd gotten boring brown eyes, whereas he had gorgeous green ones she could easily lose herself in. She looked down at her own mug to avoid his gaze. "Last night was fun. Really, *really* fun." She cleared her throat nervously. "But I don't have time for a relationship. Not that you're asking," she tacked on as she looked up at him again.

She was more or less jumping to conclusions, but he'd hinted more than once that he wouldn't mind taking her out. And from what she'd heard around town—directly from his sister-in-law-to-be—it wasn't like he was a serial dater. In fact, he didn't seem to date anyone at all.

Besides, no way in hell was she getting involved with someone in law enforcement. Not when she was in WITSEC. It was simply too complicated.

She didn't do complicated anymore. She'd made the mistake of telling someone that she was in the program years ago—someone she thought she'd loved, though looking back, she now knew that she'd just been desperate for a connection. He'd been a charmer, a useless man who knew how to say the right things. Thankfully she'd seen through him—eventually—but she wasn't making that mistake again.

She'd been moved by her handler immediately—in the middle of the night. They'd come in, gotten everything in one swoop as if she'd never lived there at all. She hadn't been able to say goodbye to anyone. Her handler had been extremely disappointed in her, but thankfully understanding. Autumn had sworn never to do something like that again and they'd given her a second chance. Nine years later, she hadn't screwed up since then.

"So you're shutting us down before we even have a chance at anything? Because I would like to take you out on a date. More than one. Just so we're clear on that. I want more than sex, Autumn. Though I want that too."

She stared into his eyes for a long moment, trying to find her voice. She hated to say no, but she had to make the hard choice. Had to draw that line. "It's not a good idea," she whispered. Before he could respond, she stepped forward, crossing the distance between them because she didn't want things to be weirder than they had to be at this point. "Look, I swear it's not you. I know that sounds like a jackass thing to say. I just... I don't have room in my life for anything complex."

"I'm a very simple man. I have *very* simple needs," he murmured again, his eyes dropping to her mouth.

A shudder rolled through her at the heat in his expression. She wanted to throw caution to the wind but... "I want to be friends. We're *neighbors.*"

She could tell he wanted to argue, but after a long moment, he nodded. Then, surprising her, he kissed her on the forehead before sighing. "We can definitely be friends. And as your neighbor, if you need any help around here, you know all you have to do is ask."

There he went again being wonderful and perfect. Her friend Serenity was getting married to Lincoln's brother, Lucas. She always talked about how wonderful her fiancé was. Maybe the Jordan brothers were all wonderful. Because they were all good-looking and all incredibly kind.

Instead of acting like a jerk after she'd told him she wasn't interested in more, he was actually being a damn grown-up. Which, perversely, made her decision a whole lot harder. She'd thought she'd be able to keep him at a distance easily now, had expected him to argue that he didn't want just a fling. Instead he was being... Mature. *Damn it.*

"Well, friends make each other breakfast," she said. "Are you hungry? I've got a dozen eggs and enough stuff to make a really cheesy omelet."

His mouth curved up slightly even as he shook his head. "I've actually got to take care of a few things today and promised my mom I'd stop by the ranch."

She nodded because it was probably better that they made a clean cut like this. And she had a feeling that if he hung out here any longer this morning, they were both going to end up naked again, no matter what she'd just said. Which would just complicate things even more and make her look like a flake.

Taking her by surprise, he kissed her again, this time softly on the mouth, but she leaned into it without conscious thought—because she was drawn to him like a magnet—before he pulled back. Then he murmured something about going to grab his clothes, and she felt like a giant dick.

When she heard scratching at the back door, she let Shadow in right as Lincoln joined her in the kitchen. "At least take your coffee with you. You can return the mug to me later," she said.

Nodding, he plucked it from the countertop as Shadow whined softly, trailing after him.

Yeah, she felt the same—she didn't actually want him to leave but it was for the best. Something she was going to have to remind herself of probably a hundred times today alone.

At her front door, he paused, his expression somber. "I'm serious, if you need anything around here, just let me know. No strings attached."

Her chest tightened as she looked up at him. She hated that things couldn't be different—that she would always have secrets to keep. And if she really dwelled on it, she could admit she hated some things about her life, that all her choices had been taken away from her. But she refused to fall down that rabbit hole ever again. Refused to feel sorry for herself. She was lucky to be alive. Lucky to have this chance at all. "I will. Promise."

After he left, she sat on the floor against the door as Shadow jumped into her lap, kissing her face. She felt as if she'd just made a huge mistake but she simply didn't think it was in the cards for her to ever be in a real relationship. And definitely not with someone in law enforcement.

Just... no.

When she heard a familiar ringtone coming from the kitchen, all her muscles pulled taut. It was the ringtone of her handler with the US Marshals. If Erica was calling, that was not a good thing. They rarely checked in with each other anymore.

But Erica had very likely seen the news. Autumn had avoided being seen by any of the media but they might be able to get her picture if they dug hard enough. She didn't have an official picture listed on the school website and she had no social media accounts. Still, she could have been listed as one of the people who had been at the bank robbery.

At that thought, ice coated her veins. She wanted to see if the news had listed her as someone who'd been at the bank during the robbery. If they'd shown her face on any of the feeds, or if there were clips online... that would not be good.

When the ringing stopped, she told herself that she would call her handler back later. She simply didn't have the mental fortitude to deal with anything right now. Not after sending Lincoln away.

Not after another damn disappointment in her life.

Quickly, she turned on the news, hoping for a peek at something regarding the bank robbery and praying that they didn't randomly show her face. She would also check online, doing a heavy search for any mentions of the robbery. That was where the real worry was, online.

She didn't want to move again. Hell, she *refused* to move again. She'd finally found a place she loved, finally had friends and a place that felt like home. No one was driving her out of her home again.

CHAPTER FOUR

Rand Coventry opened his eyes at the click of the infirmary door unlocking, then opening.

"Son," his father murmured as he approached the bed. As usual, his father wore a custom suit, but the jacket seemed to hang slightly today and his cheekbones were sharper than normal.

He swallowed hard and pressed the button on the bed so that he could sit up slightly, ignoring the discomfort in his side as he moved. He was on an IV drip—morphine maybe, but he wasn't sure because he could still feel a bit of pain.

"I'll see that the warden loses his job," his father growled as he pulled up a chair next to the bed.

Rand shook his head, or tried to, but it was too much effort. Once upon a time, his father had actually had enough clout to make something like that happen. He'd had judges in his pockets, men who mattered. All that had changed a decade ago.

Everything had been ruined because of Ana Diaz and her big mouth. She should have taken a bribe... or hell, she should be dead.

"It's fine," he rasped out even though rage surged through him. He was *always* angry, had been angry for ten years straight. He smothered it, hid it from everyone as best he could, but he didn't belong in prison. And he

definitely hadn't deserved to get stabbed over a basketball. But here he was, lying in the prison infirmary, lucky
the slice hadn't been a few inches to the right and nicked
his kidney. At least it was better than his cell—even if he
did have a cell to himself.

"I don't understand what happened, how you ended
up in the general population." His father patted his hand
gently but that was his only outward demonstration of
affection. They weren't technically allowed to touch anyway. Though the guard standing at the windowed door
didn't make a move to stop his father from putting his
hand on Rand, at least.

He flicked his gaze back to his father. Ten years ago,
Tom Coventry had been a state senator, had been moving up in his political career and had been on the fast
track to become a US senator. Now his father worked for
a hedge fund, and he did well for himself, but it had
never been his father's dream. And Rand hated the Diaz
bitch for taking *that* from his family as well.

She'd ruined everything.

"It was a stupid mistake," he said, even though he
wasn't sure it was a mistake at all. He might've pissed off
the wrong people. Who knew? At this point, he didn't
even care anymore. All he knew was that he did *not* want
to spend the next twenty years in a prison cell. Death
would be better. "Doesn't matter," he muttered and
closed his eyes.

"It does matter," his father snarled, the show of heat
and emotion surprising him. He opened his eyes as his
father leaned forward. "I haven't forgotten, and if it takes

me until I die, I will get justice," his father whispered, barely loud enough for him to hear.

His father's rage-filled words fed his soul. Rand had thought that his dad had given up on trying to find her. The guard couldn't hear them, but his father's words were vague enough that Rand understood what he meant. She'd been in witness protection since the night she'd escaped what should have been a quick death.

Ten. Long. Years.

She'd been in hiding. Living her life while he was locked up in a six-by-eight cell with someone telling him when to eat, when to sleep, when to shower. Nothing in his life was his own.

He pressed the button again so he could sit up a little farther. The guard at the door knocked once and made a motion for his father to step back.

His father's jaw tightened but he did as ordered, and sat down.

"How's work?" Rand asked, knowing they couldn't talk openly about the bitch. Not when it was likely everything was being recorded.

"It's going well."

"How's Mother?" He hadn't seen his mom since he'd been arrested. She'd divorced his father, changed her last name and moved to the East Coast, far away from California.

"I have no idea. Last I heard she was shacked up with some mechanic in South Carolina."

That surprised Rand, but he didn't respond. He wasn't even sure if it was true. It was impossible to imagine the proper, conservative woman who'd raised him living with some blue-collar asshole who fixed cars for a living.

He knew he shouldn't ask about his mother—she'd abandoned him when he'd needed her most. Had called him a psychopath for not being remotely sorry about what he'd done.

Well, he still wasn't sorry, because he'd done nothing wrong. That whore had wanted what he'd done to her. It wasn't his fault she'd overdosed. *Stupid.* That was what she'd been. A stupid, stupid woman. He'd tried to explain all of that to his mother, to get her to see his side. But she'd simply stared at him in horror.

Rand tried to banish the image of his mother looking at him with such... disgust, before she'd walked out on him the last time. His hands had been chained to the table, had rattled incessantly as he'd tried to lunge after her, to make her understand.

"Try and get better," his father said as he stood. "I'm going to see about getting you transferred again."

He'd already been transferred to three different prisons. It was impossible to keep what he'd done a secret. Not that anyone cared about him raping and killing a woman. Though the word "rape" was bullshit. But that was what he'd been accused of. No, they just didn't like that he was rich, that he'd been born privileged. That he came from one of California's wealthiest families.

It wasn't his fault, but everyone in prison hated him for it, and he suffered for it daily.

Rand simply nodded at his father and pressed the button so the bed went back down. Even this little communication had taken so much energy out of him.

Though nothing would ever extinguish the raging fire burning in his chest. Nothing, until he had his fingers wrapped around Ana Diaz's throat, until he'd snuffed the life out of her completely. He wanted her to beg for mercy, beg for him to spare her. But he wouldn't. She had to suffer for what she'd done to him and his family.

"I meant what I said," his father said as the guard started unlocking the door again. "I will make things right. I will locate the problem if it's the last thing I do."

The problem. That was a good word for her. A problem.

One that needed to be stomped out of existence like the cockroach she was.

CHAPTER FIVE

Autumn stepped into Tailwaggers Grooming, a pet grooming place owned by her friends Serenity and Adeline.

Adeline was working the register when she stepped in. Wearing a purple T-shirt with an image of a tapdancing pug on the front and a sparkly purple headband, she looked completely on brand, making Autumn grin.

"Hey, surprised to see you out front. And I'm digging the headband." It was Saturday and no surprise, they were bustling.

Two women were over at the stand that sold locally made dog treats, and every DIY grooming stall was full with people who didn't have enough space at their own homes, washing their dogs here.

Autumn had more than enough room, but this was one of her luxuries—she got Shadow groomed fairly regularly. She could wash Shadow herself but her sweet pooch hated getting a bath and hated getting her hair cut, and Autumn didn't like dealing with it. So this way she was never the bad guy with her sweet girl.

"One of the girls called in sick so I'm pulling double duty. And thanks, I got them in every color of the rainbow." Grinning, Adeline patted her dark curls. "Shadow should be ready, if you give me just a second," she said as she looked at the computer and typed something.

At the sound of the bell jingling overhead, Autumn glanced over her shoulder, then froze.

Lincoln.

She hadn't seen him in nearly two weeks, and she wasn't sure if he was actually avoiding her or if it was just dumb luck. She'd been busy with the start of the new school year and he always worked long hours, so it wasn't really a surprise that she hadn't seen him around the neighborhood.

What she *was* surprised about was that she missed seeing him so much. Okay, she couldn't even lie to herself. *Occasionally,* she peeked out her window when she heard him come home. And she *might* sometimes watch him and his fine ass walk to the mailbox every afternoon. His uniform was made of the ugliest polyester on the planet but he made it look good. In fact, it was ridiculous how much so.

"Lincoln, hey," she said. Why did her voice have to come out all breathy? Oh God, she could feel her cheeks flushing as she turned to face him fully.

"Hey," he said, quickly closing the distance between them. "How are you?"

"Good. How are you?" she asked awkwardly, even as she internally cursed herself. She sounded like a moron.

"Good." A long silence stretched between them. He glanced at her mouth once, the heat flaring in his gaze a surprise, but he quickly recovered and cleared his throat. "Are you picking up Shadow?"

"Yeah. What are you doing here? Did you finally get a dog?" He'd mentioned that he'd been thinking about getting a rescue.

"No. I'm picking Daisy up for Lucas, since he's working late. Serenity said she was ready."

She nodded once and stood there, basically clasping her fingers together in front of herself. She forced herself to drop her hands as she scraped the recesses of her brain for something, *anything*, to say. "So... I haven't seen you around lately." *Way to state the obvious, dumbass,* she cursed herself again.

"Yeah, I've been working crazy hours." His jaw ticked, and he looked as awkward as she felt.

So at least there was that. Ugh. They never should have slept together. Because now she knew exactly how he sounded when he climaxed—exactly what kind of things he said in bed. And she very distinctly remembered the feel of him holding tightly onto her hips as he'd pounded into her from behind—the third time. And then that fourth time when he'd given her multiple orgasms with his mouth, then his cock. Gah. She inwardly screamed at herself. She had to stop thinking about him naked.

As they stood there staring at each other, she tried to think of something to say. They'd been so damn mature before, but after not seeing him for weeks, she was feeling beyond awkward. Clearly so was he. *Think of something normal to say!*

She was vaguely aware of the back door opening, and thankfully Serenity strode out with Daisy on a leash. The shepherd mix with gorgeous brown eyes pranced toward them, her tail wagging happily to see Lincoln.

And more than a bit of relief slid through her when he took the dog, saving them from more awkward standing around.

"Thank you so much for this!" Serenity said. "Sorry to run, but I'm slammed in the back." She gave Autumn a quick smile too before hurrying to the back again.

"Well, I'll see you around," he said before heading out.

She managed to force a smile and stepped back as the two women who'd been shopping stepped up and paid for their purchases. Once they were gone, she found Adeline watching her expectantly.

"Oh, right. Let me pay for Shadow before you get her. It'll make things easier." She pulled out cash, but Adeline still stood there.

Her friend glanced over her shoulder, but no one was paying attention to them and the place was loud with barks and water running. "I'll grab your girl in a second," Adeline said. "But first... What's up with you and the sexy sheriff?"

Autumn could feel her cheeks warming up and cursed how reactive she was. "What are you talking about? We're neighbors."

"I would say that you guys are definitely *more* than neighbors. You've been wanting to hit that forever."

She let out a startled burst of laughter. "I've literally never used those words."

Adeline raised an eyebrow. "Maybe not, but I know you."

No, you don't. No one does.

"So what's up with you two? That was the most painful, awkward interaction I've ever seen in my life. I literally had secondhand embarrassment watching that."

She groaned and lay her head on the glass countertop. "I don't want to tell you."

"Oh my God, did you guys finally sleep together? Was it horrible? I've never heard anyone talk about him dating. I guess I just assumed that since he was so hot, he knew what he was doing in the bedroom."

She lifted her head and glared at her friend. "It wasn't bad. It was *incredible.* We sort of... got together after the bank robbery. I was feeling really out of sorts that night and... then I jumped him. And we had a whole lot of sex." *So. Much. Sex.*

"And?"

"That's it. I've barely seen him since."

Adeline blinked in surprise. "He just ghosted you? What a dick."

"No! He... He said he wouldn't mind taking me out on a date. In fact, he sort of insinuated he wanted to date me, but I'm just not looking for a relationship. I told him I wanted to be friends."

"Friends?" Adeline arched an eyebrow. "Sounds suuuppper fun."

"All right, that's enough out of you, smartass. So what time are we meeting up tonight?"

"I can pick you up at six thirty if that's still good for you?"

"Definitely. And speaking of sex or dating or whatever, when are you going to tell who you've been sneaking around with?"

To her surprise, a faint sheen of pink flushed Adeline's light brown skin. "I'm not sneaking around with anyone."

"Really? You've been so covert lately."

Adeline lifted a shoulder. "I'm... interested in someone but it doesn't matter. He doesn't know I exist." She glanced over her shoulder then turned back around. "Let me go grab Shadow. We really are crazy," she said just as three people walked in, presumably to pick up their pets.

"Okay, but you're going to give me all the details tonight," she said as she pulled out her wallet to pay.

Ten minutes later as she headed down Main Street with Shadow in the backseat, happily wagging her tail as she looked out the window, Autumn had the strangest sensation well up in her belly.

Almost like... she was being watched.

She knew she was just being paranoid, letting old fears swell up and choke her. Rand Coventry was still in jail, and after the robbery a couple weeks ago, her handler had subtly made sure that any mention of her or any picture of her was squashed. She wasn't sure how the marshals had done it, but Autumn was grateful.

Still, the last two weeks, there'd been a weird sensation pressing on her.

Dread. That was it.

As if she was simply waiting for the other shoe to drop at some point.

Some part of her felt like Verona Bay was too good, that this whole setup—her living situation, her job that actually gave her fulfillment, her friends—it was all too good to be true. Which was another reason she was keeping Lincoln at arm's length. In her experience, if you got everything you wanted, or hoped too much for a better future, it was all yanked away.

It was why she regretted her decision to not give Lincoln a chance, why she kept thinking about the what-ifs. What if they got together and she told him the truth? And then what if it didn't work out? She'd very likely have to move again. Or what if they got together and she never told him? There would always be a lie hanging between them. She hated the thought of that too. No successful relationship could be based on a lie. And yes, her "lie" would be literally keeping her alive, but it's still felt wrong somehow to keep a huge part of herself from Lincoln.

Of course, she was getting ahead of herself, because it wasn't like they had an actual relationship, but... Something told her that if she opened up her heart to Lincoln Jordan, she was never getting it back. Like ever.

Sighing, she shelved all thoughts of sexy Lincoln and dismissed the weird sensation of dread. She was simply getting caught up in her head. If she didn't stop now, she would fall down another rabbit hole and spiral.

She was going out with her friends tonight and she was going to enjoy herself. The first couple weeks of school had been fun and incredibly busy, as always. The kids were on their best behavior, excited to see their friends again and everybody loved her class. In art, they could express themselves, have fun. She knew they all thought of her classes as their "easy class" but every year she got a couple kids who she knew would enjoy art for the rest of their lives.

That made it all worth it. So even though she'd given up on her dream of making a living by being an artist, at least she knew she was making a difference in her community.

As she pulled into her driveway, Autumn saw something on her front porch. She had security cameras and a security system, but her phone had been tucked into her purse and she hadn't heard an alert from the camera.

Not bothering to check the video, she parked in her garage then hurried to the front porch to find a little bag. It had a Tailwaggers sticker on it. When she opened it and saw some treats for Shadow, plus a note, her heart skipped a beat as she read it. *Got these for Shadow.* —*Lincoln*

It was a simple message with nothing superfluous at all, but the gesture itself, the small gift warmed her from the inside out.

Lincoln had stayed true to his word and hadn't pressured her for anything more. No dates, nothing. She found herself simultaneously relieved and disappointed.

After the raw, hot sex they'd shared—and enough orgasms to fry her brain cells—she was craving him. Just another taste wouldn't hurt. And as she heard her own stupid thoughts, she realized she sounded like an addict. Ugh. It wasn't too far from the truth. Now that she knew what Lincoln was capable of, it was hard not to obsess about him.

She mentally shook herself and hurried back to the garage to shut it before going inside. She'd heard Lincoln's car coming in at random hours over the last two weeks and knew he was working seriously long days and nights. Autumn had also heard talk that he was working with the FBI in regards to the two bank robbers.

Even though she told herself that she didn't need to reciprocate his gift—and she knew he wouldn't expect a thing—she still wanted to do something for him as well.

As a friendly neighbor *only*.

"Yeah right," she muttered to herself, earning a glance from Shadow, who was devouring the treat she'd given her.

So after a quick check of her cupboards, she made him a small batch of her special chocolate buttercream cupcakes. She also made an extra one for herself and left it out, because if she was going to all the trouble of making cupcakes, she was going to certainly enjoy one herself.

She would just leave them on his doorstep. He should be home soon, given the late hour, so they should be all right for now.

As she crossed her front yard to take them to him, he pulled into the driveway. Dammit. It was too late to turn around and run now. She would look like a total weirdo. Besides, they needed to move past the awkwardness and he'd taken the first step with the thoughtful dog treats.

He parked in the driveway instead of his garage and jumped out, immediately heading toward her in long, powerful strides. "Hey, everything okay?"

The sun was setting, and would be down in about twenty minutes, but there was still enough light to see him perfectly clearly. Seriously, polyester never looked so good. His broad shoulders strained against the tan-colored button-down shirt, and she knew for a fact that he looked even better *without* that shirt.

"Everything's good. I wanted to say thank you for the dog treats and was just dropping this off for you." She held up the cupcake carrier. "Are you off for the night?"

"Just for a few hours. It's been a weird couple weeks," he said, his gaze falling to the little carrier. She had them in multiple sizes and different colors, a white elephant gift from the teachers' party last Christmas season. She held out the plastic container with the blue handle. "What is that?"

"Chocolate buttercream cupcakes."

He let out a groan of appreciation, one that sounded very similar to the way he'd groaned as he'd buried his face against her neck. "Thank you. That's really thoughtful."

"Well, the dog treats were really sweet."

His brow furrowed even as he took the gift. "You didn't have to return the gift."

"I wanted to. You've been working crazy hours and besides, we're neighbors, *friends*," she added.

His eyes went all molten for a moment and she wondered if they could ever be truly friends after what they'd shared together. Then he cleared his throat and gave her a half smile she felt all the way to her core. "Thank you. It's been a hell of a day and it's nice to come home to this." Butterflies went wild in her stomach as she returned his smile. In that moment, she wished that he came home to *her* every night. After losing everything, she could admit that she craved a real family, a sense of stability and belonging. But wanting something too much— and did she ever want Lincoln—was a recipe for disaster. "Well, I hope your night gets better."

He simply nodded and gave her another heated look. She wondered if he was even aware of the way he watched her. Because he didn't do it with anyone else that she'd seen. He was usually so good at wearing a neutral mask, but sometimes there was a... longing in his gaze.

One she felt mirrored inside her. She wanted...

Well, it didn't matter what she wanted, did it?

She cleared her throat. "I'm meeting up with some girlfriends to go see a movie tonight." She shouldn't be telling him anything, shouldn't be inviting him further into her life, and she told the voice in her head to shut the hell up. "So I may be getting in late."

"I'll keep an eye on your house."

"Thanks." She took a step backward, needing distance for her own sanity. "Enjoy the cupcakes."

"I will."

She finally made it back inside her house, and as she leaned against the closed front door, Shadow jumped up on her thighs, furiously shaking her head, begging for pets.

Crouching down, she buried her face against Shadow's neck. "I'm such a fool," she murmured to her dog. Such a stupid fool.

Shadow attacked her face, licking and kissing her as if she hadn't just seen her five minutes ago. It was impossible not to smile under such affection, so for now, Autumn shelved her wayward thoughts about Lincoln and headed to her room to get ready.

This might not be the life she'd wanted, but she had to make the best of the hand she'd been dealt.

CHAPTER SIX

Six weeks later

Autumn glanced through the peephole of her front door instead of checking the video camera on her phone at the sudden knock. No one randomly stopped by her house. For a moment she thought it might be Lincoln. The last six weeks they'd seen more of each other and things had been friendly—if still occasionally awkward because of the simmering attraction between them. The attraction she was continuing to ignore.

Or trying to. Desperately.

When she saw Derek Ryman on the other side of her door, however, ice coated her entire body, crawling up her arms, gripping her around the neck as she tried to drag in a breath.

No.

There was another knock. "Autumn?" he called out. He rubbed a hand over his dark buzz cut as he glanced around.

She couldn't ignore him, even if she wanted to. Taking a deep breath, she tugged the door open. "What's wrong?" There weren't many reasons for a US Marshal to show up on her doorstep unannounced. And of the actual reasons, none of them were good. He was Erica's partner, but Derek wasn't Autumn's handler, so she was surprised he was here without Erica.

He casually glanced around before pinning her with his dark eyes. He had a five o'clock shadow and looked exhausted, slight circles under his eyes. "Can we talk inside?"

Wordlessly, Autumn stepped back and allowed him into her home. He'd only been here once, over a year ago. He was big, like Lincoln, and took up a lot of space.

"So what's going on?" She certainly didn't want to make small talk.

Thankfully he didn't want to either. He never did. He motioned for her to sit in her living room and since her knees were feeling wobbly, she did just that.

He sat on the leather love seat across from her, pushing aside one of her teal pillows with a dancing llama on the front. His long legs jutted out as he tried to get comfortable, but he gave up quickly and leaned forward. "There have been a few more newsfeeds about what happened. Those two jackasses are getting more attention since they haven't been caught yet."

"The bank robbers?"

He nodded once, his jaw tight. "Yes. We managed to scrub almost every mention of you in particular but a few photos of you slipped through. They were taken from the side and grainy. We've since scrubbed them but they were out there temporarily. It was on two really small news feeds from a couple small towns along the coast."

"I haven't seen anything." She'd been paying attention too, more or less obsessing over it. "And I haven't heard from any friends that they saw me on the news." That was something that friends would naturally bring up. She would if she saw one of her friends on the news.

"Like I said, it was very brief and the news didn't come out of Verona Bay, but a couple towns away. Still, Verona Bay is getting more attention because of the bank robbery and because of what happened not too long ago."

She knew exactly what he was talking about. Her friend Serenity had been kidnapped by a serial killer eight years ago, and her twin sister killed. The lunatic had been working with a partner who had seen fit to stalk Serenity once she'd moved back to Verona Bay. The partner had kidnapped and unfortunately killed people in Verona Bay only months ago. The town had bounced back, but there was still a feeling of unease in the air. And they'd been spotlighted nationally. Autumn hadn't been because she hadn't been involved in any of it, but still. It had put Verona Bay on the map, so to speak.

"I'm not moving," she said bluntly. She figured that was why Derek was here in person—to tell her that it might be a possibility. So she wanted to save anymore small talk and let him know his trip was wasted.

"Look, Autumn—"

"No. Is that why Erica isn't here? Did she think you could bully me into moving?" She had to agree to move, and there had to be a real and present threat. There were so many damn rules with the program, and she'd read the WITSEC book thoroughly.

"No, she's getting someone else settled right now. We're pulled pretty thin at the moment and she knew you wouldn't respond well to a new face. It's why she sent me."

"That doesn't make me feel any better."

"Look, you're secure. We haven't had any viable threats against you—any threats at all. There's been absolutely no chatter about you. I don't even know that he is a threat to you anymore, but if something happens and pictures of you are leaked and someone figures out who you are, you need to be aware that a move could be imminent. We've never lost anyone who followed the rules, and I'm not going to start now." His jaw was set firmly as he watched her.

"I've followed every single rule—"

He cleared his throat slightly.

"Except that *one* time. I was twenty-three and stupid. And I've learned my lesson." Boy, had she ever. "I'll never make that mistake again. And I'm not moving," she stressed. They needed to be clear on that point.

"Just be careful, pay attention to your surroundings. I know you know all this but I wanted to talk to you in person. I just wanted you to know that there is a slight chance you might have to move again."

She stood, her spine straightening. "I don't know another way to say this, Derek. I will *not* leave Verona Bay. Besides, I thought he got stabbed or something. The news insinuated that he might die." She kept tabs on Rand Coventry, covertly of course.

Derek jerked in his seat. "Did you do a search for him?"

"Yes, but I used a proxy and I was careful with the wording." Because she knew that certain type of searches could trigger an alert if someone had traps set up to search for other people's online searches. The US Marshals had gone over all of this with her and she took her safety very seriously. The fact that someone might be able to track her because of a search online was terrifying. It was a scary world, knowing what hackers could do.

Frowning, he finally stood. "If I call you, make sure you answer." A demand, not a request.

Which was fair, since she'd ignored his last call. But he hadn't left a message so she'd assumed it hadn't been an emergency. "I will. But I need you to hear what I'm saying because I won't change my mind." Not this time. Not after the life-changing thing she'd just found out.

He simply sighed and opened her front door before stepping out onto the front porch.

All Autumn's stomach muscles tightened when she saw Lincoln standing in front of his mailbox. Oh, hell. He paused, looking over at the two of them, and then he glanced at the car in her driveway. He waved at her and she waved back, hoping he didn't think she had some random guy over.

He lingered by his mailbox, very clearly taking his time as Derek strode to his vehicle and drove away.

Lincoln walked over to see her as soon as Derek was gone, and she didn't miss the way he watched the back of the car, likely memorizing the license plate. She wasn't even sure why she thought he might do that, but he was a cop through and through. "Everything okay over here?" he asked cautiously.

"Yeah, I'm good. Just an old friend stopped by."

He watched her carefully, and she knew her body language probably screamed that she was tense and uncomfortable as she shoved her hands into her oversized cardigan sweater. "He just had bad news, that's all."

He paused, as if weighing her words, then nodded. "If you need anything, let me know. I'm home the rest of the night."

"I will, thanks." As he headed back to his house, her fingers skated over the pregnancy test in her pocket. Sighing, she pulled it out and looked at it again.

Still double lines. Still pregnant.

She needed to tell Lincoln. She'd just found out herself today and needed to confirm with her doctor before she gave him the news, but... This was the third test she'd taken, and they'd all come back positive. They'd used condoms—a lot of them—but clearly one of them had failed.

She was pregnant and didn't know how the hell she was going to tell her impossibly sexy neighbor that he was going to be a father.

This changed everything.

CHAPTER SEVEN

As he jogged down the quiet street parallel to his own, Lincoln couldn't get rid of the uneasy feeling in his stomach. He'd been working with the FBI the last few weeks because the Feds had thought the bank robbers had doubled back. Which they had, but the two brothers—Justin and Calvin Martin—had been caught finally. Unfortunately the bastards had escaped custody because of a glitch in security, something he'd just learned today. Now the brothers were in the wind and could be anywhere.

That wasn't the only thing bothering him, however. He could admit that he'd been annoyed seeing that guy leave Autumn's house earlier.

Especially because he could objectively state that the guy was good-looking, in his late thirties, maybe early forties, and he had the walk of someone with law enforcement or military experience. Not to mention the man had definitely been carrying a weapon. The bulk had been small but he'd been wearing a jacket that was slightly heavier than normal for September in Florida.

Yes, it was unseasonably cool this month, but... Something about the guy had been off.

Maybe Lincoln's feelings for Autumn were muddying his view, but he didn't think so. He'd memorized the license plate but wasn't sure what he was going to do with that. He wasn't in the habit of checking up on his neighbors and he never abused his power. But Autumn's body language had been way too tense. She'd looked almost... scared, and she hadn't shared what the bad news had been. A death? A threat of some sort?

Hell, he was letting his mind run away from him.

As he rounded the corner onto the next street, he nearly jerked to a halt when he saw Autumn up ahead, Shadow trotting along in front of her. Seeing her was a balm to his soul.

In tight purple running pants, rainbow-colored sneakers, and a black racer tank, she was a bright pop of color against the neighborhood. Everything about her was that way, however. At least for him—he could never take his eyes off her if they were in the same room. Her dark hair was pulled back into a ponytail and it was clear she was distractedly listening to her iPod as she walked.

When she looked over and saw him, she smiled and, even from twenty yards away, the sight of it made his heart skip a beat.

He increased his pace, covering the distance quickly to meet up with them. "Hey, I didn't know you jogged."

She snorted as she tugged out her earbuds. "I just wear the cute clothes. I'm more of a walker, and it's good for Shadow. She's the only reason I'm out, actually. She absolutely loves her afternoon walks—and I get to listen to audiobooks. But if I had to choose, I prefer Pilates and short aerobic workouts."

Autumn seemed a lot more relaxed right now as they talked. That was a relief.

Shadow, clearly not getting enough attention, jumped up on Lincoln's legs, her tail wagging wildly. "I'm sorry about that." She tugged on her, pulling the dog back down.

"It's okay," he said, laughing as he petted the Border Collie.

"I've got her signed up for some obedience classes. She's pretty good about listening but she doesn't need to be jumping up on people."

He crouched down and scratched behind Shadow's ears. "It's all good, I promise, but obedience classes sound like a good idea. She's young anyway. It usually takes them until about three years old until they truly settle down."

"You know a lot about dogs?"

He nodded and fell in step with her, his jog forgotten. He would much rather walk with her anyway. "Oh yeah, we grew up with a bunch of them. I really do want to get one but... With my schedule, it just wouldn't be fair right now. I don't want to get one until I can fully commit to taking care of it." He was hoping to hire a new deputy soon and be able to offset some of his shifts. But that all depended on their budget and federal funding.

"That's very responsible of you," she said, giving him what he could only describe as a strange look. She was watching him very carefully, as if he were a bug under a microscope.

He wasn't sure what to make of that look so he ignored it. "So how's school this year?"

"Good. A great group of kids signed up for art this year, and I've taken to teaching even more classes downtown at the cultural center." She paused, and glanced at him. "They've actually offered me a full-time job."

"Wow, that's great." The cultural center was ninety percent funded with grants, run impeccably, and a huge benefit to Verona Bay and the surrounding area.

She nodded as they stepped up onto the sidewalk, walking even closer together given the size of the sidewalk compared to the road.

"Are you going to take it?"

"I honestly don't know. I'm kinda shocked by the offer, but also pleased. There's a lot of pro-conning in my future. It's not like they've said I have to take it or lose my classes. I'll still get to do those even if I turn down the offer. But the thought of working there full time is pretty great."

"Well if you ever want to talk it over, I'm here." He wanted to be more than a sounding board for her, and it was taking everything in him to ignore his natural instinct to pursue her. But he knew that pushing her would be the biggest mistake. He knew that she wanted him—physically at least—and he was willing to be patient. And his pursuit of her would be more subtle. If he wanted to win her over, he had to be patient. Good thing the military had taught him to be just that.

"Thank you," she said, giving him that odd look again. It was a searching look, as if she was trying to figure something out.

"Everything okay?" he asked, wondering if it had to do with that guy he'd seen at her house earlier. He wanted to ask about it, but didn't want to sound like a jealous jackass.

She cleared her throat and looked ahead of them, watching Shadow intently. "Yep. So how did you like the cupcakes?"

"I'm ashamed to say that I ate all of them. I thought about sharing them down at the office, but decided to keep them for myself. They lasted two days in my house." Barely.

She let out a startled burst of laughter and damn if he didn't love the sound of it. She should laugh often, and always around him. God, this woman had him so twisted up. As they reached her house, he tried to think of something else to say but kept coming up blank.

"Hey, I've been meaning to tell you," she said, pausing in front of her house. "I'm going to be having a deck put in soon so I'll let you know when the construction starts. It'll be normal work hours, but I'll still let you know."

"Who'd you hire?"

"I actually haven't hired anyone yet. I've just been getting some estimates."

"I can do it with Lucas and Easton. Hell, we can do it for you for just the cost of materials, I'm sure. I'll have some of the tools, but Lucas will definitely have everything we need." His brother ran his own successful construction company, and might even have leftover materials she could use.

She shook her head, her dark ponytail swishing slightly. "No way. I'm not going to take advantage of my friend's fiancé, or you, my neighbor."

"How about I take advantage of him then? He can afford it, trust me. And Easton won't mind at all. Buy him a six pack and some pizza and he'll be fine."

She snorted softly. "I'm sure your brothers would love that you're offering them up for free labor. I'll think about it," she added when it was clear he was going to say more.

"That sounds a whole lot like a no."

"I *promise* I will think about it."

It still sounded like a no, but he wasn't going to push it, even if he had this driving urge to take care of her. To protect her. "All right. See you later." He watched her walk into her house even as the weight pushed against his chest again.

Hell. He'd never wanted a woman as much as he wanted her. She called to him on every level, and even though it was clear she actually did want to be friends, it was also clear that there was a very real wall between them.

One he would do anything to break down.

CHAPTER EIGHT

Lincoln answered his phone immediately when he saw his brother Easton's name on the caller ID. "Hey, what's up?"

"You busy?" Easton's tone was uncharacteristically sober. Of the three Jordan boys, Easton was definitely the fun-loving one—the best big brother.

"I'm at work but not out on a call. Is this work-related?" His brother was a firefighter and since it was Wednesday, Easton wasn't on shift right now as far as Lincoln knew.

"Maybe. I mean not officially right now, but... I was talking to Mac Collins and he's worried about one of his brothers. The youngest."

"Joe, right?" Mac was the same age as Lincoln, but he'd been an absolute hell-raiser all through high school and one year after. Then he'd joined the Marines, gotten his life together, and after his parents died, he'd come back to take care of his younger brothers instead of reenlisting. Easton and Mac were part of a fishing club, however, so they were friends even with the age difference.

"I guess he went out flounder gigging with some friends and hasn't come back."

"Where's Mac at now?"

"His shop."

71

Lincoln glanced at his watch. It was five and he was on shift for a couple more hours. "I'll head over there now. Should I call him or..."

"I'll let him know you're on the way. Thank you."

"No problem. Will I see you at Sunday dinner?"

"You know I wouldn't miss it." They often had Sunday dinner at their parents' house when all of their schedules would allow. Lately it hadn't happened, but this Sunday they were all miraculously off.

Once they disconnected, he called out to Ellen Harris, his new admin assistant. "Heading out."

"Official call?"

"Not sure yet. I've got my radio and phone on me." That was the thing about smaller towns, sometimes people wanted things official and sometimes they didn't. But because he knew almost everyone and the majority of town had his personal cell phone number, he got random calls at all hours of the night. Sometimes he had to turn the volume off and just know that if there was a true emergency, that the station would call his radio. Otherwise he would never get any sleep. *Ever.*

The drive to Mac's place didn't take long and he found the man's 1968 Bronco sitting in front of his workshop. Collins owned his own furniture-making business—his woodworking skills were incredible and he sold pieces internationally. He also occasionally did custom jobs for Lincoln's brother, Lucas. Lucas hired him whenever he could get him but the man was often booked up too far in advance. The Mac of today was a far cry from the wild boy Lincoln had grown up with.

Before he'd even gotten out of his car, the front door opened. Mac strode out, tugging his gloves off. "Thanks for coming by."

"So what's going on?"

Mac held open the glass door for him, locking up behind him as they both entered the quiet studio. "Maybe I'm just being a worried big brother. And now I have a lot more respect for the terror I was to my parents. Joe went out gigging for flounder with some friends last night and told me he'd be late. Said he'd be in by two, likely."

"Have you talked to his friends?"

He nodded, his expression grim. "Yeah. They've all come back. They said he wanted to stay out a little bit longer, and one of them hinted that he might have been meeting up with a girl he's been seeing afterward. But he's not answering his phone, and he must have turned it off because our family locator app is turned off as well." He rubbed a big hand over his buzz haircut, his jaw flexing once. "He's a good kid. Not like me at that age. *Both* my brothers are good kids. I'm not too strict and I respect their autonomy. They come home when they say they will and if they're going to be late, they call or text me. They know that's the only real stipulation I have with them still living at the house."

"Joe's eighteen, Mac." He was a grown man, not a kid, so it changed things from a legal standpoint.

"I know I can't file a missing person's report yet because of his age."

"That doesn't mean we can't do anything. Do you know what area he was gigging in? What boat was he on? And do you know the name of the girl he was supposed to be meeting up with?"

The tension in Mac's shoulders eased and he quickly gave Lincoln all the information.

"I'll reach out to all the local fishermen, call the marinas and tell them to keep an eye out for him. And I'll go talk to the girl."

"She's a few years older than him. She's twenty-three, not exactly a girl." Mac's mouth curved up slightly as he shook his head. "My brother apparently has more game than both me and Dylan."

Lincoln simply snorted and headed out, already making the first phone call by the time he'd made it to his cruiser.

The probability was high that Joe had hooked up with the woman he'd been seeing and turned off his phone because he was having too much fun. But on the chance that wasn't the case, Lincoln was going to do his due diligence. He looked out for his town, loved Verona Bay. They'd seen enough tragedy recently, and he sure as hell didn't want them to see any more.

CHAPTER NINE

"That was a great class everybody," Autumn said as she stepped away from her own easel. She taught at the cultural community center two nights a week and over the summer she taught week-long classes. Not every single week, but for most of the summer. It was a good way to give back to the community that had embraced her, do something she loved—and she got paid for it.

Plus the people in charge of the center had been very accommodating about not using her photograph in any online type of advertisements. She'd simply had to tell the director of the board that she had an ongoing stalker issue and that was that. And it wasn't very far from the truth.

"Pretty sure my llama looks more like a yak," Serenity said as she started cleaning her brushes.

Autumn stepped around and looked at her friend's colorful painting. She blinked once, and bit back a grin. "As long as you had fun, that's all that matters."

"So no comforting words that all art is beautiful?" Serenity raised her dark eyebrows as she started drying her cleaned brushes.

Autumn snickered. "I was going to say it looks like a cross between a dolphin and a yak. You know you're only here for the free wine anyway."

Serenity let out a startled laugh. "It's true. Pretty sure even Harper wouldn't let me hang this monstrosity in her room."

"Now that kid has some talent," Autumn said, as around them, people started packing up to head out. Everyone was so good about cleaning up so while she'd have to stay afterward to tidy things, it would require minimal effort before she could head home. It was one of the reasons she didn't mind teaching mid-week on a Wednesday.

Though tonight she'd been distracted, trying to wrap her mind around being pregnant—and everything that entailed, including telling Lincoln. She'd just found out, so she wasn't keeping it from him, but she couldn't figure out a good way to say "hey, I'm preggo and you're the father." Ugh.

"She loved the classes she took this summer with you and has been begging me to put her in something after school. I swore I would never overwhelm her with extracurricular activities but she's been pushing hard for this."

"The classes I teach now are too advanced for her but I can recommend a couple really great instructors here for her age group."

"Thanks, I'll text or email you later."

She nodded, smiling and moving on to Adeline's painting, which was... incredible. She'd apparently eschewed tonight's theme of animals and gone with a Verona Bay sunset. The water was choppy and wild and she'd used shades of gold to give it a sparkling effect.

"This is amazing," she murmured. "Really, really good. I didn't realize you painted so well."

Adeline shrugged. "My mom was into painting." She paused, cleared her throat, and Autumn thought she might continue down that path, but then she said, "You feel like going to grab a drink or pie after you finish up?"

"I want to say yes, but I'm pretty beat from the day. And I've got to pick Shadow up from my neighbor's. She's having a puppy date this evening." She also had to get up fairly early for school tomorrow. Another reason she was thinking of taking the job offered by the cultural center; the flexible hours. They were a little bit later—which would be nice. She'd also get to bring Shadow with her to work on occasion, which would be really great. But... she now had a bun in the oven and had things to think about, like healthcare. It was a little bit too much to worry about right this moment, however. Especially since she needed to talk to Lincoln first.

"I get it, and thanks for another good class. I had fun tonight. But I *really* want to paint nudes. And I can think of some perfect models we could get in here."

"You're just a pervert."

Lifting a shoulder, Adeline grinned. "I'm not saying you're wrong."

Shaking her head, she moved on to Maris Carson—a wonderful woman in her late forties who ran a shelter for abused women. She'd painted an adorable cluster of flamingos with blue and purple feathers instead of pink. It was whimsical, something the world needed more of.

"I shouldn't have favorites, but I love this," she murmured to her friend.

"I do too," Maris said matter-of-factly. "I think I'm going to hang this in my office. So are we still on for next month?"

"I'll be there—as long as you bring that biscotti." She was kidding, she'd be there regardless, but Maris had brought her homemade biscotti to the last painting class Autumn had taught at the shelter and it had been mouthwateringly delicious.

"Sounds like a fair deal. I'll be by tomorrow to pick up my painting." Maris gave her a quick hug, then hurried out.

She spoke to a few more people as they packed up and before long, it was just Autumn and a math teacher from the school. Stella was standing in front of her canvas, slightly trembling as she knocked over her cup of paintbrushes.

Autumn hurried over and stilled her when she tried to pick them up. "Don't worry about the brushes. I've got this. Are you feeling okay?" she asked, even as she guided her to a seat at the table behind the canvases.

Stella didn't protest, just collapsed into one of the chairs. "I just got an alert on my phone that those bank robbers escaped."

Stella had been there at the bank that day with Autumn and the others. Autumn knew about that, Lincoln had already told her. "The Feds will catch them," she said, reaching out and squeezing her hands in her own. "They know who they are now and have their faces, so they'll be recognized or caught on camera."

"What if they come back?" Stella asked, her dark eyes wide.

"To Verona Bay? Why on earth would they do that? No way, these guys are going to head north, I guarantee it. They're long gone from Florida." Or at least she hoped so.

Stella nodded but then started trembling, taking in shallow, unsteady breaths.

Oh hell. Autumn recognized a panic attack when she saw one. "Come on, bend over a little bit more and put your head between your legs. Take a deep breath." As Stella did, Autumn hurried to her desk and grabbed her cell phone. Instead of calling the station, she called Lincoln, who thankfully picked up immediately. The man was a steady rock.

"Hey, what's up?"

"Are you working tonight?"

"I was just about to leave the station."

"I'm down at the cultural center and Stella is having a bit of a panic attack about those guys escaping." The sheriff's station was only a few blocks away. "Maybe if you talk to her... I don't know, it might make her feel better," she whispered the last part. "I hate to put this on you but she's known you a long time." She'd actually been Lincoln's math teacher, and while Autumn genuinely liked the older woman, she didn't know her well.

"I'm on my way."

She set her phone down and hurried back to Stella, who was now sitting up straight, her breathing steadier. Her dark eyes were more focused now as well.

"You want some water? Or maybe soda?" The sugar would probably be good for her.

"Coke would be good."

By the time she'd grabbed one from the employees-only area and made it back into the room, Lincoln was already there, not in uniform. So he really must've been about to leave, or maybe he'd even already been on his way home.

He really was good at what he did, had worked incredibly hard to foster a trust of law enforcement in this town, something that wasn't common everywhere. He was one of the good ones, and when she saw the concern on his face as he crouched down in front of his former math teacher, warmth spread through her chest. It was impossible not to like this man, to respect him, to think about what kind of father he would be...

Oh, no. She wasn't letting her head go there.

Or her heart. She had too much to deal with right now to let wild emotions get involved.

Autumn hung back quietly as Lincoln talked to Stella, expertly calming her down. She'd heard through the grapevine that he had experience negotiating with terrorists—something that both horrified and impressed her.

He'd been in the Marines, she thought, or one of the military branches. She'd gone out of her way *not* to learn too many things about him because the more she learned, the more intrigued she was. A few of the women she worked with had huge crushes on him, which was just annoying because they talked about him on occasion. When they'd found out Autumn lived next door to him, they'd talked about coming by to see him, which had made all of her hackles rise. And this was all *before* she'd actually slept with the man. She had no reason to feel territorial about him.

She started gathering up all the paintbrushes and cups, emptying out the dirty water and putting everything up while Stella and Lincoln quietly murmured in the corner. She figured that Stella would want privacy anyway, and as someone who hated being the center of attention, she understood.

"I'll be back in a minute." Lincoln's delicious voice wrapped around her, making her turn as he headed to the door with Stella, who seemed much better now.

Stella waved at her as they headed out. As Autumn was finishing up and drying her hands, Lincoln stepped back inside. In dark jeans and a T-shirt with the logo of a past music festival on it, he looked younger than he did when in uniform. More approachable. She understood why the women in town thought he was attractive—she certainly wasn't immune. It was weird, he was the youngest of the Jordan brothers, but didn't fit the mold of youngest. From what she'd seen, he was more serious compared to Easton, a man who was like a big puppy dog, always smiling and joking.

"I think she's okay now," he said quietly.

"Thank you for stopping by. I know that's not exactly law-enforcement territory but... I didn't really know what else to do. I figured it would make her feel better to hear from you that those guys would be caught."

"They will be. They never should've gotten out in the first place," he muttered. "How much longer do you have? I'll walk you out."

"I'm pretty much done and just need to lock up at this point. But..." She cleared her throat as she tried to think of how to tell him what she *really* needed to tell him. There really was no easy way to say "hey I'm pregnant and you're going to be a father." Nope, no easy way to say that. She was just going to have to rip off the Band-Aid. She had no idea how he would react, if he would want to be involved... and she didn't even want to guess. She needed to tell him and then figure things out based on his reaction.

"What's wrong?" He'd moved through the tables and chairs in mere moments, his movements economical and stealthy. Frowning, he studied her and reached out, as if he might touch her, but just as quickly he drew his hand back. "You look a little pale."

"I'm fine. I need to talk to you about something. It's... I just... I'm pregnant."

CHAPTER TEN

L incoln stared at Autumn as he digested her words. "Can you repeat that?"

She shoved out a breath, color returning to her face as she gave him a wry smile. "Sorry, I thought saying it quickly would be best. I'm pregnant. And you are the father, in case that wasn't clear."

He blinked, looking into her dark brown, amber-flecked eyes. "Wow. Okay."

"I know it's a lot to take in."

Hell yeah it was. "You're sure you're pregnant?" Inwardly, he cursed himself. Of course she was sure. This was... a lot to deal with.

She nodded and absently picked up a hand towel that was stained every color of the rainbow. She ran it through her fingers over and over, clearly nervous. "I took a couple tests when I realized that I'd missed my period. I've always been kind of spotty anyway, but... It had been a solid two weeks so I was getting kind of worried. All the tests were positive, and I just saw the doctor earlier today. She confirmed it. I'd planned to tell you tomorrow, but since you're here, I figured there was no sense in waiting any longer. Now I feel like I'm rambling, so please say something."

"What did the doctor say? Is there anything special you need to be doing? Should you be working around paints? Not that I'm criticizing anything you're doing right now. I just want to make sure we're on the same page." This was huge news, and he was certain it would hit him later just how huge. For now, he didn't want his response to something so big to be something she would hate forever. He was in shock, yeah, but he imagined she had to be too. This wasn't something they'd planned.

She blinked once before narrowing her gaze at him. "I'm fine being around these paints... You don't want to take a paternity test or anything?"

"No. Unless it makes you feel better." He might not know her as well as he wanted to, but he was good at reading people. Autumn wouldn't lie about this.

"I don't need one. I have no doubt that you're the father. I just thought... I don't know, that you'd want to be sure." She wrapped her arms around herself.

He wished he had the right to touch her, to comfort her. "Well first of all, I believe you. Second, I've never seen random guys staying at your house. I mean, I guess you could be..." He cleared his throat, realizing he didn't want or need to voice that thought. "We'll do whatever you want."

"I'm keeping it," she blurted, as if he hadn't figured that out.

"I kind of figured, since you're telling me." Which meant that they had a lot of decisions to make.

"Okay then. I don't... I don't actually know what else to say right now. I never got further than telling you I was pregnant in my rehearsed conversations."

"You rehearsed telling me?"

Her mouth curved up slightly. "Like a million times in my head today."

"One of those condoms must have broken," he murmured. They'd used quite a few. He'd never really thought about being a dad. He'd assumed that one day he would want to be, but only with the right person.

Autumn is the right person.

That thought flared in his mind but he quickly suppressed it.

"So..." She seemed to flounder as she watched him. He was in the same boat, having no idea what to say. He just knew that he didn't want to be a giant dick.

"When's your next appointment?"

"Why?"

"Ah, because I would like to go with you to the doctor—if you want me to be with you. I want to be involved with everything." This wasn't what he'd planned for his life, but if she was pregnant, then he'd been fifty-percent involved in making that happen. And he would step up every way he could and hopefully ease her load some. He wanted to be completely involved but didn't want to overwhelm her with questions about the future—because the truth was, he was overwhelmed as it was.

She blinked at him again.

"Are you so surprised?"

"Kind of, yeah. I don't know, in my experience, men are..."

His jaw tightened. "Whatever experience you've had, it sounds like those guys suck. Look, I want to be as involved as you want me to be. This is definitely a *lot* to take in but we'll face it together. You won't be alone in this." The protectiveness he'd always had for her grew inside him—and the most caveman part of him wanted to tell her that they should get married. Which was stupid, he knew that. She had all sorts of walls between them and wasn't letting them down anytime soon. Maybe not ever. It didn't matter what he wanted.

When her eyes welled with tears, she quickly dashed them away and waved him off when he stepped forward to pull her into a hug. "I'm fine. I promise. And I'm not normally a crier."

"That might change during pregnancy. I have enough cousins to know," he said dryly. "Apparently there's something called pregnancy brain that is very real." God, his parents were going to be ecstatic. Even if he and Autumn weren't together—though he wished they were— his mom especially had the biggest heart of most people he knew. She would be so happy to add someone else to the family.

She laughed lightly, and he let the sound wrap around him. "Honestly, I don't even know what to do right now," she said. "I just can't believe how well you're taking this. I've gotten so worked up in my head that this was going to be an awful conversation."

"I'm glad that I'm so scary."

She laughed again, the tension in her shoulders easing. "It's not that, I swear."

"Look, do you want to head to the diner and talk for a while?" It would be good for them to be seen around town together anyway, especially when it came out that they were having a baby together. They would need to talk about future plans—childcare options, custody stuff. Ugh. He hated the thought of things being split up.

"That sounds pretty amazing."

"Are you really done here? I can help you clean up if not." He glanced around the studio, taking in all the painted canvases.

"Nope, I'm done. I just need to grab my purse."

As she did, it hit him full force that holy shit, he was going to be a father. And he wasn't horrified. Maybe a little nervous. Kids could be scary. But, wow. His brain was trying to catch up with the news. His mom would certainly be excited to become a grandmother—she'd been badgering Lucas not so subtly.

Lincoln felt... hell, he wasn't sure what he felt. He liked Autumn a whole lot. More than he'd ever liked a woman, and he wanted the chance to get to know her more. This had changed everything.

But it hadn't changed his desire for her. Nope. If anything, he knew he was going to have to fight his protective urges even more. Autumn was not the kind of woman to put up with bullshit. Now he was even more determined to win her over.

"You're starting to look a little green around the gills," Autumn said as she slid up next to him, purse over her tan shoulder.

Tonight she had on a loose multitiered skirt and a lacy white top with barely there straps. The straps of her pastel blue bra were visible underneath and she had on custom-made jewelry from one of the local artisans. He recognized the style because he'd been living here forever. Her arms were bare, showing off her many tattoos—some dipping below her top so he couldn't see them fully now. But he knew exactly what they looked like. He'd seen, kissed, ran his teeth over all of them. She'd left her long dark hair down today and it fell around her heart-shaped face in soft waves. Right now, she looked different than she did when dressed for teaching—more at ease, casual, in her element.

"I'm just digesting everything," he said honestly. "And I'm thinking how happy my family will be."

She shot him another look of surprise, her pretty eyes widening. "Happy?"

"I think you seriously underestimate how much my mother wants another grandchild." Because Louise Jordan had officially "adopted" Harper as her own grandchild even though Serenity and Lucas weren't married yet. She'd made it clear she wanted more grandkids to spoil.

Autumn watched him cautiously, and he didn't blame her.

Holy shit, he... was going to be a father.

CHAPTER ELEVEN

Autumn opened her eyes, disoriented by the shifting shadows of her bedroom.

She heard something breaking. *Glass.* She paused, confused as she pushed her comforter off. Wait... why was glass breaking? And where was Shadow?

She jolted slightly as reality sank in. Someone was breaking into her place!

Heart hammering, she shoved her covers fully off and jumped out of bed onto quiet feet. She had to run, *hide.*

She ducked into the hallway, shadows twisting and turning everywhere.

The hallway seemed to stretch on for an eternity in front of her. What was happening? Why was she here?

Run, the voice whispered in her ear. *Run, or you will end up just like me in the dumpster.*

Sweat pouring down her back, Autumn's heart was a staccato beat in her chest as she started running down her hallway. The harder she ran, the longer it grew in front of her, the end of it turning into the overstretched mouth of a laughing clown, elongating out like a macabre funhouse.

She sucked in a breath and sat up in bed, her *real* bed, as the nightmare faded around her. She took in her surroundings and found Shadow crawling up next to her, whining softly as she watched Autumn.

Reaching out, she dug her fingers into her fur and petted her gently. Shadow settled immediately even as Autumn leaned forward, her breathing still erratic.

It had just been a dream. Or a nightmare. The beginnings of one, at least. She hadn't dreamt about her old place in ages, hadn't had a nightmare in years. She hadn't even thought about that little one-bedroom apartment she used to live in. She had more to lose now, maybe that was the reason for the unease, the nightmare.

Shuddering, she got out of bed and stripped off her short pajama set. Her entire body was slicked with sweat so she hurried to the shower, not caring that it was four in the morning. She wouldn't be going back to sleep anytime soon. She could get a little painting in anyway this morning after a quick shower and coffee.

No, damn it, she couldn't have coffee anymore, she remembered.

Decaf it would be—even if it was a sad substitute for what she really wanted. The trade-off was worth it though.

Until she'd seen those two lines on the pregnancy test, she hadn't even realized she wanted to become a mother. And when her doctor had told her that, yes, she was absolutely pregnant, she'd been nervous but also overjoyed. Something that surprised the heck out of her.

She loved the kids who she worked with at the high school and the kids of all ages that she taught at the cultural center. But she'd never thought becoming a mother was in the cards for her.

She'd never seen herself settling down with anyone, starting a family. Her own family had been small and broken. She was terrified of being a mother, but Lincoln's reaction had been something she could only have dreamed of. She knew he had to be beyond shocked, but he hadn't been dismissive or anything. At the diner, he'd had all sorts of questions she hadn't even thought of—what would they do for childcare, how would they split up custody.

Somehow, he was handling things better than her. She wished... she really wished things were different between them. Because when he'd been asking her those questions, she'd imagined that they had a life together, a house together, that they did all those parenting things as a team. Which, she knew that you didn't have to be married to be a good team, but still... he made her want things for herself she'd never thought would happen.

As the water pulsed over her, she tried to shake off the remnants of her nightmare but it had transported her back to the night a masked man had broken into her apartment and tried to kill her. She'd barely escaped out the window with her life, jumping down to the second floor using the fire escape and racing off into the night on bare feet. She'd been lucky, there had been a taxi driver who'd been idling on the street while eating a sandwich. He'd whisked her off to safety and, after that, she'd gone into witness protection.

The marshals hadn't been able to prove that the Coventrys had sent someone after her, but the threat had been real enough that no one believed it had been a coincidence. The man who had broken in had worn gloves and a mask, but he'd cut himself on the glass he'd shattered. They'd been able to identify him from his DNA—but he'd been dead when they'd found him in his shitty one-bedroom apartment.

He'd died of an overdose but the evidence said it hadn't been self-inflicted. If it had been the Coventrys behind it, they'd made a mistake in choosing such a moron. She hadn't been willing to stake her life on them making the same mistake twice. And she hadn't wanted to live the rest of her life looking over her shoulder, either.

After that incident, she'd been under protective detail 24/7 until after the trial. Which had ended up being a lot shorter than anyone predicted—because of her testimony and the pictures she'd provided. Rand Coventry had been heavily advised to take a deal after her testimony.

But she didn't want to think about Rand Coventry right now. Or his father, with his cold, angry eyes; the state senator who'd watched her as if she was scum, when in reality his son had been the monster.

Nope, there was no time for that in her life. She was Autumn Perez now. She lived in Verona Bay, she had a job she loved, friends she loved, and she was about to be a mom.

She was having a baby with her sexy next-door neighbor—and more confused than ever. She wasn't going to let the past drown her.

Still… the nightmare had unnerved her enough that she double checked that her alarm system was set once she got out of the shower. And triple checked her locks.

She wished she could tell Lincoln about her past, wished she could confide in him at least a little, but knew she wasn't allowed. No, she had to keep her past a secret. It was the only way to stay safe.

CHAPTER TWELVE

A n alert on Ezra's computer made him look up from his bowl of pot stickers. He had five screens surrounding him but at the insistent beeping, he looked at the one on the far right. He was working multiple jobs, always was. He'd grown up poor and had been hustling since he was fourteen. Some things never changed—except now he made considerably more for his efforts and he didn't answer to anyone.

Now he took anything that not only paid the bills, but allowed him to create a nest egg. A very large one in many offshore accounts.

"What have we here?" he murmured to himself as he set the bowl down, the food almost immediately forgotten.

Normally he didn't eat in here, but his fiancée had knocked earlier, insisting he take the food. He took it only to please her—because she pleased him very much. But he hadn't allowed her inside. He never did. He didn't allow anyone in his domain, not even the woman he was going to marry. She lived here, shared every part of his beachfront home, but not his office.

As he quickly scanned the text, he frowned. The alert was from an old job, one he'd long since forgotten about. He'd picked this one up on one of the dark web forums he frequented, hoping to locate the woman the client wanted eliminated. But it had gone cold, as many jobs did. Especially since this particular one had allegedly gone into WITSEC.

For the most part, he didn't screw around with that. It was far too much work to mess around with protected witnesses with not enough return on investment—usually, anyway. And once they went into the system, he usually shelved the jobs. There were far too many easy jobs he could take locating people who thought they could disappear on their own with all sorts of ill-gotten gains. But without the help of professionals to assist them, they were easily found. Well, easy by his standards. He'd been hacking since he was eleven and he was very, very good at uncovering secrets.

As he looked at the alert from the facial recognition software he often ran in the background, he leaned back in his chair.

A twenty-four percent match.

Not very good. It was the side of a woman's face, taken from a news story in nowheres-ville Florida. Hmm. Still, the job was live, had never been taken down. It wouldn't hurt to dig a little into this...

His fingers flew across the screen, alternating with the voice commands he gave it.

Then he paused. "Verona Bay," he murmured to himself. The name was familiar, but he couldn't imagine why. He'd never been there. He didn't care for the East Coast—too humid. Miami was the only exception because he liked the nightlife and beaches, so he occasionally spent winters there.

It took him a moment but then he remembered why the name of the small town sounded familiar. Another couple quick online searches revealed what he was looking for.

Dozens of articles about a serial killer—linked to infamous serial killer Michael Black—ran across his screen. *That's right,* he thought. He remembered seeing it in the news feeds months ago. Lately the country was such a dumpster fire of chaos, however, that this incident had been quickly forgotten.

A bloodhound on the scent, Ezra ordered his program to do a search for any picture or article mentioning Verona Bay that might be a potential match to the current picture he had a twenty-four percent match on. It didn't take long before another one came back with a thirty percent match to the target from ten years ago. It was a picture of a woman wearing a hoodie and jeans, clustered with a group of other people. It had been taken in the midst of one of the searches for a dead woman.

There was another picture he'd snatched from social media. The picture hadn't even been private, though his program would have picked it up regardless.

He grouped the pictures together to attempt to create a better image of the woman. The target.

Now his program deemed that this could very well be a fifty-six percent match.

Ezra leaned back again and pondered his options. Before contacting the client, he needed eyes on the ground, needed a much better picture of the woman—needed a *location.* It would cost him some money upfront. He debated if he even wanted to waste his time or not. He didn't need the money, but he did want a new Lamborghini.

Stretching back in his chair, his gaze flicked over to one of his perimeter security screens. His fiancée was talking to one of the gardeners. He narrowed his gaze, not liking the way the man was looking at her in her string bikini.

Annoyed, he texted Tony, someone he used for small jobs, even as he kept an eye on her. *You busy?*

The response came back 30 seconds later. *Yes but if you need me for a job I can do it.*

It's easy money. Just need a picture of target. A crystal-clear one. Because there were some things that he couldn't get online, especially since it didn't appear as if this woman had an online presence. Not from what he'd been able to find.

I can leave tonight. Send me the details.

You'll see it in ten minutes. He would send it via the secure forum they used for all transactions.

How much?

Ezra snorted, not surprised Tony hadn't asked the price first. The man was more than decent at what he did, but he wasn't that bright. *Ten thousand plus expenses and transportation.*

He received a thumbs up emoji back and smiled.

Considering this job was a couple hundred thousand a few years ago, he didn't mind parting with ten grand to make sure he had the right person. If he ended up being wrong, well, no risk, no reward, something he believed in thoroughly. He'd just have to eat the money if it wasn't the target.

His gaze flicked back to the screen where the guy—who should be working—was *still* talking to his woman. At least she looked annoyed. But he still didn't have to like it.

He sent a message through the other forum, wondering if the client even checked it anymore. It had been almost a decade, after all. Considering who the client was, something told Ezra that this job was still open.

Once he was done, he shoved up from his chair. It was time to remind the asshole hitting on his female who was boss.

* * *

Tony hated going into jobs blind like this. He didn't have any sort of frame of reference for where to find his target. His only instructions were to get a picture of a woman who might be living in Verona Bay, Florida.

And the picture had to be crystal clear. He had an expensive, long-range camera, but he usually got up close and personal to take the important pictures, so he mostly used his phone. The picture itself had to match using some sort of facial recognition software. The odds of him finding a woman in a town, even a small one, weren't great. But he'd done it before.

He was also going to do some reconnaissance for Ezra and see about getting cameras set up around town. In small places like Verona Bay, there weren't CCTVs everywhere like in New York or Miami. If there had been, Ezra wouldn't have needed Tony at all.

Tony was used to grunt work like this, and he didn't mind it. The pay was good enough to cover all his bills, afford him a small house that he owned, and he got to travel some. It wasn't like he had a reason to be home anyway. His kids didn't see him anymore, not since their mom had died.

Sighing to himself as he drove down Main Street in the small town of Verona Bay, he shelved thoughts of the family who would have nothing to do with him.

It was time for him to get to work, and he had to be focused. Ezra wasn't a bad guy to do work for—Tony had never even met Ezra before and wasn't sure if that was his real name. But the guy always paid on time, had never tried to stiff him. And if Tony turned down a job, there were no hard feelings. He took what he could.

He parked in the quaint, coastal downtown and looked around. He'd done some basic research on the way here and there were a couple festivals coming up. It wasn't like he needed a reason to be here, but he liked to have a cover story. Especially since he wasn't sure how long he would get stuck here.

This truly was like finding a needle in a haystack. Or more like a needle in a stack of needles. He had no idea where this woman worked, nothing. What he did have was a photograph from ten years ago of a pretty college-aged student with big brown eyes and long dark hair. He didn't know who she was and he didn't care.

He was good with faces. He'd been instructed to look for an older version of this woman, get a picture of her and find out where she lived. The address was important.

Ezra had also been clear that she might not even be here in town. Tony would still get paid either way but he liked to do a good job, because he always wanted repeat business. And sometimes Ezra gave him bonuses, so he definitely wanted to find this target.

His daughter had just had a baby a year ago—and he still hadn't seen his grandson. His daughter had made it clear that he wasn't welcome around either of them. But maybe if he sent her some money, tried to smooth things over, it would make a difference.

Annoyed at himself, he shook those thoughts off again. No distractions, he reminded himself. He'd been doing this a long damn time and had only got sent up once for robbery. It had been a short stint—though long enough for his dead wife to poison his kids against him.

He'd never turned on his partners though, and he knew it was part of the reason Ezra had hired him for that first job years ago.

He kept his mouth shut and he didn't ask questions. He didn't care who this woman was, didn't care who was looking for her. Because if he knew the details, he might end up feeling sorry for her. And he liked sleeping in his king-size bed with a clear conscience at night.

Stepping out onto the sidewalk, he took in the various shops. A dog grooming place, a café, a quilting shop, a hardware store. It was like Mayberry here.

Sliding on his sunglasses, he decided to head to a nearby diner. He hadn't eaten since breakfast and people always talked openly in general, but especially when they were relaxed and eating. Usually they forgot that others could be listening because the majority of the time, people only paid attention to themselves. But sometimes he got lucky.

Glancing both ways, he paused as a sheriff's cruiser drove by, only stepping onto the road and hurrying across once it drove past him.

Luckily, Verona Bay didn't have a huge law enforcement presence. The bad thing about small towns, however, was that the cops usually knew most of the residents. And locals would easily recognize him as an outsider.

He had to be careful not to do anything to stand out, and he had to stay far away from any and all cops.

CHAPTER THIRTEEN

A deline pulled up to the front of Mac's furniture workshop and had to remind herself to keep it together when she was around him. Not that it mattered—he barely acknowledged her existence. It was... disappointing.

The man was crazy talented, his woodwork actual art in her opinion. But she was here to tutor his youngest brother, Joe. He was in community college and struggling with math—something she excelled at. At first she'd tutored him at their home, but they were having some construction done so she'd been doing it at his shop the last couple weeks. Now she saw Mac more. Normally Mac just grunted at her, barely making eye contact, but that was probably a good thing.

She had terrible taste in men, so if he actually *had* paid attention to her, she would've known that he was no good for her.

As she reached the front door, Mac strode out, looking as surprised as she felt.

"Adeline?" He paused, looking confused.

Oh God. Had he ever said her name before? She loved the way it sounded coming from this giant, bearded man who might as well be a lumberjack. Today he had on a plaid flannel shirt rolled up to his elbows, showing off roped, muscular forearms she'd had fantasies about.

That's right, *forearms*. They were drool worthy. But not as much as his piercing blue eyes, which had ensnared her from pretty much the moment they'd met. To the extent that she'd more or less stumbled over her words the first time they'd met, unable to form complete sentences.

"I'm supposed to tutor Joe today?" It came out as a question because she actually hadn't seen Joe's car in the parking lot.

"Hell, I forgot you were coming."

Well, that was a blow to her ego. Of course he'd forgotten—another reminder that he didn't know she existed. She kept her smile in place, however. Ugh, she really needed to get over this stupid crush.

"I actually don't know where Joe is," he blurted. "I have no idea what's going on with him. He hasn't returned my phone calls and it's been about thirty-six hours."

Alarm jumped inside her, everything else fading as she digested what he'd said. "That doesn't sound like him."

"No, it doesn't. I've already let Lincoln know, but there's only so much he can do because Joe is an adult. And the local fishermen have been scouring areas where he was last seen on his little dinghy." He had his keys in hand, his expression tight.

"Are you going to look for him now?"

"I've already been out, but I was going to do one last cruise looking for him before dark. I can't do nothing."

She tucked her own car keys into her jeans pocket. "I'll go with you."

He shook his head. "You don't need to do that. I mean, I know he's missing tutoring today, but I'll still pay you for your—"

"Let's just stop right there. You're not paying me for today. And I know I don't need to go, but I want to. Besides, if you're steering the boat, I can be extra eyes. It certainly won't hurt, especially if you're going to be navigating through the creeks. You might miss something."

He paused for all of a second and then nodded. "Thank you, and I really appreciate this."

"No problem." She fell in step with him and hurried toward his truck, concern for Joe increasing.

"I might be a while," he said as they reached his Bronco. "So if you want to drive separately, you should."

"I've got tomorrow off. I don't care how late we stay out. Joe's a good kid who hero-worships you. I don't think he'd stay out without a really good reason." Technically he was considered an adult, but eighteen to her still felt like a kid.

Jaw tight, he nodded and they both jumped into his Bronco.

"Look, he's dating someone..." She hedged. Joe had mentioned it to her but then had quickly asked her not to tell his big brother. Which seemed ridiculous because he was eighteen.

Mac snorted. "I'm well aware. She hasn't seen him either."

"Well, that's a dead end then," she murmured.

"He told you about Marcy?" he asked as he backed out, surprise flickering across his hard features.

"Yeah. He's quite impressed with himself for landing an older woman," she said, using air quotes. Because Marcy was all of twenty-three and fairly immature for her age in Adeline's opinion. She was a sweet girl though, even if a bit jealous, according to the stories Joe had told her.

Mac gave her a curious look before averting his gaze back to the road. "Does he talk to you about anything else? I'm not trying to pry. I just... The more I know about him." His big hands tightened on the steering wheel, his knuckles going white.

"I mean, mostly we work on math and prepping for college, but we talk about regular stuff too, I guess. He wants to impress you, I know that much. You gave up a lot for him and—"

"He said that?" He seemed alarmed by the thought.

"Well yeah. He told me how you came back to take care of him and his brother when your parents died. He's grateful." Hero worship was definitely right. He'd also confided in her that once he got his degree, he wanted to join the Marines like his big brother.

Mac's jaw tightened.

"What's wrong with that?"

"I don't want him to feel pressured or anything."

"Oh, I don't mean that he feels pressured and that he ran off or something. He's a *good* kid. A very well-rounded one, in fact. Especially for being eighteen. I certainly didn't have my head on straight when I was that young." She held back a snort as she remembered how dumb and impetuous she'd been at that age.

"Somehow I doubt that," he murmured as he pulled into the parking lot of a small marina.

She had no idea what he could mean by that.

He cleared his throat as he pulled into a parking spot close to the bait and tackle stand. "Pretty sure he has a crush on you." The words seemed to be torn from Mac as the gravel rattled under the force of his tires stopping.

She snorted softly. "He did. For maybe that first week or two. I shut him down very gently, in case you're worried. Trust me, they weren't real feelings, not puppy love even. Just a teeny bit of infatuation until he met Marcy. He really likes her." And if Marcy didn't know where Joe was...

Adeline tried to push down the worry bubbling up inside her. Even if he had a good head on his shoulders, he was still eighteen. Hopefully he'd just gone out with friends and maybe lost his phone or... no. One of his friends would have let him borrow theirs. She bit her bottom lip as more worry welled up.

"I didn't know you knew about his crush." He turned to look at her then, something she couldn't read in his blue eyes.

She lifted a shoulder. "Well, I'm a decade older than him, and it wasn't hard to pick up on his cues. He wasn't very subtle—he asked me out for coffee and a movie and made sure to know that he had money to pay and it was very much a date request." He was forthright, she'd give the kid that.

Mac's mouth pulled up slightly, amusement flickering there for an instant before the worry was back. "No, my brother is not subtle. Hell, I don't like any of this," he murmured, looking around the parking lot. "I'm... worried. I know in my gut something's wrong."

On instinct, she reached out and grabbed his hand. A jolt of something arched between them. Taken by surprise, she quickly yanked her hand back.

Whatever it was, she thought he might have felt it too but he simply looked away and hurried out of the vehicle.

She had to half jog to keep up with his long strides as they headed down the dock toward the main office—a tiny shack that housed a small fridge and a portable air conditioner so the attendant wouldn't get heat stroke during summers. After he checked in with the attendant to see if anyone had seen Joe, they hurried down the long row of docks.

As he palmed his keys, she frowned. "Shouldn't we bring food or anything? Or water? Maybe... a first-aid kit." She wasn't sure how long they would be out, and if they found Joe stranded somewhere there was a good chance he might be dehydrated.

He swore softly. "I don't know where the hell my head is. Just give me a second. My boat is in slot J-2." He motioned a few rows down to the blue and gray fishing boat. "I'm going to run to the shack and grab a few bottles of water and some snacks. I've already got a kit in the boat."

She nodded and headed to his boat, untying it as she waited for him. As she did, she said a small prayer for Joe.

The last time she'd prayed, she'd been held by a lunatic who'd wanted to murder her, and she was still alive. So maybe someone had listened—and she hoped they would again. Mac and his brothers had already lost their parents. She didn't want them to lose one of their brothers too.

CHAPTER FOURTEEN

"I think we should have at least two artists for the face painting." Autumn scanned her to-do list for the fall festival she was putting together with a bunch of business owners in town. She was involved because she worked at the cultural center and a huge part of the festival would be taking place there. All of downtown would be closed the weekend of the festival, with vendors set up in the street. She was more or less the spokesperson for the cultural center because of her relationship with so many of the local business owners downtown.

"I agree," Bianca said. "At other festivals, adults and kids both love getting that done and the lines are always too long. I think we could maybe even add a third, at least from ten to two on Saturday and Sunday, since those are historically our busiest times during the Strawberry Festival and the Christmas one."

There were murmurs of agreement before Serenity spoke, drawing everyone's attention to her. "I've been talking with the local animal shelter. I think we might be able to do something about getting some of their pets adopted as well. It'll be a great time to showcase the pets who need homes and get more interest from the community."

"That's a great idea." Autumn had rescued her own Shadow from the local shelter and they were such a great organization.

She glanced over at Adeline, who'd been uncharacteristically quiet all evening. She'd shown up late, which wasn't like her, and was now tapping her finger against the table, her gaze distant as she stared out one of the windows of the coffee shop.

Bianca had put the closed sign up to make it clear she wasn't open, though it was well past hours regardless. And with so much light in the coffee shop, Adeline was basically staring at her own reflection. Autumn didn't think she was actually seeing anything, however.

"Adeline, what's up?" She'd barely given any input over the last half hour and this new fall festival had been her idea to start with. Autumn had a lot on her mind too—obviously—and it was clear that Adeline was in the same boat.

"What?" Adeline turned to look at them, blinking as if coming out of a haze. "Yes, pets are good."

Everyone stared at her.

She sighed and shook her head slightly, her dark curls bouncing. "I'm sorry. I just have a lot on my mind."

Autumn knew that her friend had a murky past. Or at least she'd hinted at a violent ex-boyfriend. Autumn wondered if something was going on with him, but she didn't want to pry. Of all people, she appreciated privacy. Still, she reached out a hand and gently touched Adeline's forearm. "Is everything okay?"

Adeline started to nod, but then just as quickly shook her head. "No. It's... maybe nothing. But I've been tutoring Joe Collins lately, after normal work hours, and when I stopped by this afternoon, it turns out he's missing. Mac has been searching the rivers and creeks in the area but there's only so much he can cover by himself."

It was the first she'd heard of it. "Has he told Lincoln?"

Expression grim, Adeline nodded. "Yes. And it sounds like he might be doing something—he's got all the local fishermen involved anyway—but I don't know if he's going to set up an official search or anything. I'm just worried. I know Joe is eighteen, but... Well, he's *eighteen*. Kids are stupid when they're that young."

As the others asked her questions, Autumn pulled her cell phone out and texted Lincoln, asking him what was going on with Joe's search. She'd actually taught the kid his junior year of high school and he was sweet, if a little mischievous. But he wouldn't have just disappeared on his older brothers. No way.

He responded immediately. *Where are you?*

At the café. Can you tell me what's going on with Joe Collins? Adeline is really worried.

Sit tight. Be there in a minute.

She blinked at the response, then tucked her phone away. "Lincoln said he's coming over now," she said to the group.

Everyone looked at her in surprise.

"Seriously?" Adeline said.

She shrugged, feeling awkward. The sheriff's station was downtown, barely a block away from there.

Less than five minutes later, in plain clothes rather than uniform, he knocked on the door and before Autumn could move, Serenity had jumped up and grabbed the door.

"Hey, Serenity," he said, smiling at his brother's fiancée.

Autumn knew from Serenity that she and Lincoln had gone to college together, that he'd gone into law enforcement because of what had happened on campus when they'd been there, the kidnappings and Serenity's twin sister's murder.

Then Lincoln glanced at her, his gaze seeking her out immediately. He gave her a soft smile that Autumn felt all the way to her core.

They'd been texting on and off today, and even though she'd expected things to be weird between them, now that he knew she was pregnant... things had been kind of nice. Maybe still a little bit weird, but he'd stepped up in a way she simply hadn't expected. She probably should have, but she knew that people could show their true colors when you needed them most. Turned out he had—and his true colors were beautiful.

"How do you guys know about Joe?" He glanced at all of them.

Adeline quickly relayed what she'd told them.

Lincoln gave a brief nod, his jaw tight as she finished. "We're starting an official search at daybreak tomorrow. Mac is down at the station with me right now—so's his other brother Dylan. Turns out Joe and his girlfriend had a big fight before he took off, but I still don't like any of this, so we're taking this seriously. I'm going to post an announcement on the town's online dashboard and social media as well, but feel free to let people know so they can pitch in."

Adeline let out a breath of relief. "Where is everyone meeting?"

"Down at the marina. I'll be there before sunrise," he said. "I'm currently working on setting up different shifts. The local fishermen and boaters are pitching in and everyone I've called so far is helping."

"I can call in to the school and get a substitute if you need extra hands," Autumn said. "I want to help too." She hadn't dealt with any morning sickness so even though she didn't love the idea of getting on a boat, she wanted to pitch in.

"Just come after school lets out," he said. "I'm going to need people to work later shifts anyway, and I've got the first five hours in the morning completely covered."

"I'll bring a bunch of coffee and snacks down in the morning," Bianca said.

Lincoln nodded, and as the other women started talking, he motioned that he was heading out again. He hadn't needed to come in person at all, and she appreciated that he had.

Standing, she hurried outside with him, only to be blasted by a wave of warm air. It wasn't hot exactly, but she'd learned that in Florida, the humidity was nothing like on the West Coast. It was awful here some days. And she never knew what to expect no matter the time of year. Stepping outside of the air-conditioned café, she regretted wearing a cardigan.

"You don't have to come tomorrow," Lincoln said quietly, his gaze dipping to her stomach.

"Just because I'm pregnant," she whispered, even though there was absolutely no one outside this late—and yes, eight o'clock in a small town was late, "I'm not going to stop living my life. I'm fine, I promise. Please tell me you're not going to go into crazy overprotective mode."

He rubbed the back of his neck. "I can promise to *try*."

She laughed, and it felt good. "You're ridiculous." And also adorable.

"I get that a lot from my brothers." His tone was dry.

She laughed again, and realized he was watching her with a whole lot of heat simmering below the surface.

That sobered her up quickly. Her attraction to him hadn't waned at all, if anything it had increased. But she was still working through way too many things in her mind right now. Because Lincoln was the kind of guy who would absolutely propose marriage just because she was pregnant.

He hadn't yet, and she was actually kind of surprised. Probably because she'd made it clear she wanted to be friends only. Even if she wanted more, marriage for convenience wasn't happening. Shaking off those thoughts, she stepped forward and pulled him into a hug, needing human contact in that moment. More than just human contact, she wanted to touch him specifically. And something in his expression told her that he needed it too, so she gripped him tight.

He seemed surprised but he held her tight in return. The hug was wordless, something she appreciated. She wasn't even sure where her head was at right now, was still trying to come to terms with the huge change in her life—his too—and how she was going to handle the future. There were a lot of things she had to think about and decide, and she was certain she hadn't thought of them all. She hadn't even told her handler about her pregnancy—and was holding off for now.

"Thank you for coming over here," she murmured into his chest. Because she knew he'd done it simply because she'd texted.

"Anytime." She felt a whisper of a kiss against the top of her head before he pulled back. Then he was in business mode. "I've got to get back to the station. We're still ironing out the details for tomorrow."

"If you want me to come earlier, let me know. Joe's a former student there, so I have a feeling the school will be very accommodating."

"I will." He looked as if he wanted to say more, but after a pause, he simply headed out.

Butterflies were going wild inside her as she watched him hurry down the street. The man had a seriously nice ass—a perfectly sculpted one she'd held onto, bit... ugh. "Just stop it," she muttered to herself.

Somehow she tore her gaze away from him and hurried back inside to find many sets of curious eyes watching her.

Serenity spoke up first. "What is going on with you and—"

"No way." Autumn shook her head to emphasize. "Not tonight. Seriously." She had no idea what to say about what was going on with her and Lincoln. She'd told him she was pregnant because he was the father, but she wanted to wait to tell everyone else until after the first trimester. Or maybe even after she started to show.

Bianca simply snorted but looked back down at their massive to-do list for the festival. "Autumn's right, we have a lot of work to do."

Bianca had gotten sort of a reputation as a mean girl, but Autumn found that more and more lately, she really liked the other woman. Especially right now, when she absolutely didn't want to talk about Lincoln. Soon enough it would come out that she was pregnant with his baby, but not today.

CHAPTER FIFTEEN

R and instinctively tugged on his prisoner's chains as the sheriff's van cruised down the quiet highway. It was early, with streaks of orange and pink lighting up the sky. He was getting moved. *Again.* Apparently his father had actually been able to pull some strings, which surprised him. He'd likely be to his new "home" by lunch.

His father might not have gone deeper into politics as he'd wanted, but the old man had certainly made a lot of money and contacts over the years. He'd also kept a lot of the same friends, even if they didn't publicly embrace him. Somehow his father just kept getting richer and richer.

Rand still couldn't believe his mom hadn't stuck around, hadn't weathered everything with them. He gritted his teeth as he thought about her, worthless bitch. She'd abandoned Rand, and her own husband. A husband who'd given her an incredible lifestyle.

"Hey," the guy across the aisle from him whispered.

Rand ignored him. He had no clue who he was, other than he was some pervert who liked kids. No way in hell would he throw in his lot with a loser like that. He hated that they were even in the same van, breathing the same air.

The loser was getting transferred because he'd been attacked multiple times at the previous jail.

Jaw tight, he looked out the window at the passing desert. It was desolate out here, a vast nothingness stretching on as far as the eye could see. Rocks and cactuses were the only things breaking up the scenery. The arms of the slender saguaros curved upward, giving the appearance of hundreds of tall aliens dotting the landscape.

The pedo tried to get Rand's attention again, jingling his chains, but Rand continued to ignore him. He'd gotten really good at ignoring people over the last decade. He liked to pretend he wasn't in prison, that he didn't live in a tiny cell, that his life wasn't complete shit.

He'd lost *everything* in an instant. The woman he'd been engaged to had split from him immediately. He'd cheated on her and she'd stayed, but once his life became a scandal, she'd left him for "being a monster"—her words.

He wasn't sure who she thought she was fooling. She wouldn't have left him if the scandal had been different. She'd been with him for the lifestyle he could provide her, so he didn't actually blame her. He would have traded her in for a newer model in fifteen or so years anyway. Or he would have done what his father did before his mother left him—kept a younger woman on the side. That was simply how things worked.

Closing his eyes, he leaned his head back against the uncomfortable, chipped pleather seat. If he focused hard enough, he could pretend that he was on a beach somewhere, the sound of seagulls in the distance, waves crashing peacefully all around him, no tourists to bother him because it was a private beach.

"No way," one of the guys up front said, interrupting his daydream. "He's not signing with them."

They were talking about football or... something. He didn't follow sports anymore, didn't care anymore. Since he'd been tossed into prison, he'd stopped caring about most things. Only a handful of friends had come to visit him, and only in the first year. After that, all had stopped, his former fraternity completely distancing themselves from him. They were just like him though. The difference was, he'd gotten caught, had made a mistake in giving her so many drugs.

The district attorney had tried to make it sound like he'd raped her, forced her. It wasn't his fault she hadn't been able to handle partying with him. If she hadn't wanted to party, she shouldn't have come to his frat house at all.

Rand realized that his fists were clenched into tight balls, and he forced himself to breathe out slowly. He had to keep a level head, stay focused. He was going to a new prison now. That always meant "new rules", so to speak. He would have to figure out who was in charge, who to become allies with. He needed to have a certain number of allies. He was glad his father had moved him, while at the same time he dreaded having to start all over again.

"What the hell," one of the guys up front muttered.

He shifted slightly, leaning forward to see. But there was a big gate separating the two guards from him and the loser next to him. While the guards were up front snacking on stale Doritos, Rand and this loser were chained up in the back.

"It looks like their tire blew out," the guy in the passenger seat said.

He didn't know these guys, they weren't from his prison, but hired drivers. He'd been thinking of them as Fatass and Dumbass. The names were interchangeable since both men were fat-asses.

"What the hell!" the driver, aka Fatass, shouted right before an explosion rocked the air.

Rand jerked wildly under the impact, his head slamming into the window with enough force to rattle him.

Black spots danced in front of his eyes as he tried to hold on to consciousness. Pain fractured his skull as darkness edged his vision. What was that? Gunfire?

He blinked as the vehicle jerked again. Lurching forward, he tried to grab onto the bar in front of him, but the chains restrained him and he slammed into the window again.

He cried out as a wave of blackness pulled him under. He tried to keep his eyes open, tried to stay awake. He could *never* let his guard down. Could never close his eyes and expect to remain unscathed. That was something he knew well. Something the last ten years had taught him.

That was all Ana Diaz's fault.

Stay awake he ordered himself, but the darkness sucked him under.

CHAPTER SIXTEEN

Adeline chugged the last of her coffee and placed it in her cupholder before getting out of her vehicle. The sun was just peeking over the horizon, sending out streaks of purples and yellows dancing across the cloudless sky. Not surprising, the parking lot at the marina was already packed even this early. She loved that people cared, even as she hated that this was necessary at all.

Joe was still missing. And with every passing hour, it seemed more and more like something terrible had happened.

She tugged on her hiking backpack-cooler combo and by the time she made it to where everyone was gathered on one of the docks, her gaze was immediately drawn to Mac. His jaw was tight, his arms crossed over his chest as he talked to a petite brunette wearing cargo pants and a tank top. She vaguely recognized the woman, thought she might work in marine life rescue or something in one of the local labs.

"Hey." Serenity sidled up next to her, a to-go coffee cup in hand. Steam curled off the top, little wisps of white twisting into the muggy air. Lucas was right next to her, holding a matching cup. Somehow the man looked wide awake this early.

She smiled at both of them. "Hey guys. I didn't realize you were coming too," she said to Lucas, because she'd known her friend and business partner had been coming. He ran a successful construction company that was always busy.

"Yeah, my mom's getting Harper off to school today so we got here as early as we could."

His mom, Louise, was always helping out—she'd been after Lucas to make his move on Serenity long before they'd finally gotten together.

"Louise is going to be up here as soon as she gets her to school," Serenity said, leaning her head on Lucas's shoulder.

Adeline was glad her best friend had given Lucas a chance. The two of them were a sweet couple, and of all people, Serenity deserved some damn peace and happiness in life.

Feeling as if someone was watching her, she glanced over and made eye contact with Mac. He'd always been kind of brusque with her until yesterday afternoon. He murmured something to the woman he was talking to and hurried over to them in long, even strides. He had on jeans, a flannel shirt—of course—and a permanently worried expression.

Lucas and he clapped hands quickly in a sort of "guy handshake" before he lasered in on Adeline. "You want to ride with me?"

Though she was surprised by his question, she nodded. "Of course. I'll do whatever I can to help. How's Dylan holding up?"

He glanced over his shoulder, and she followed his gaze to where his other brother was talking to a friend, his hands shoved in his pockets. Joe's girlfriend Marcy was with him too, her eyes puffy and red. "Okay I think. He's riding with Lincoln."

"We'll find him. He's going to turn up at a friend's place, or…" She cleared her throat, because she knew life wasn't like that. Life had taught her that the hard way. Going against her instinct, she reached out and squeezed his arm gently. "We'll find him." She certainly hoped so.

He simply nodded, holding her gaze for a long moment before Lincoln interrupted everyone.

"Everyone, thank you for coming out today!" he called out using a bullhorn. "We found Joe's boat just an hour ago."

She sucked in a breath at Lincoln's words, and a quick glance at Mac told her that he'd already known.

Oh God. That couldn't be good.

"We've figured out who is going where so we don't cover the same area twice. Everyone will work with a buddy. Two or more people together at all times. We've also called in aerial help, so don't be surprised if you see a helicopter overhead." He started going over details as she broke away with Mac, heading toward his little boat.

Lucas and Serenity were joining another local fisherman, so she gave her friend a quick wave.

It had been a little cooler this morning, so she'd brought a light windbreaker, and her backpack was full of snacks and water just in case. She never wanted to get stranded somewhere. Mac had clearly done the same thing, she saw as soon they got into the fishing boat. His duffel bag was bigger than hers, and he had a separate cooler and first-aid kit.

There wasn't much to say as he started the engine and steered away from the dock, so she sat in the front as he maneuvered through the connected waterways, heading to wherever Lincoln had designated that they search. She didn't fish or anything but she had been out on a few different boat rides with friends over the years. Usually to go skiing out in one of the bigger lakes, and occasionally kayaking along some of the creeks. But she sure as heck wasn't a pro.

It was clear that Mac knew exactly what he was doing, however, as he expertly steered through some hanging underbrush into what turned out to be a wider part of one of the creeks. She'd never been this deep into one of the side creeks before and had assumed that this area was a dead end.

"Did the cops find anything in Joe's boat?" she asked as he slowed, steering around the jutting roots of cypress trees. His engine was a gentle hum, and she could hear others nearby, though she couldn't see anyone.

"His cell phone," Mac said quietly, the fear in his eyes real. "A lifejacket, though not his. It looks like it was maybe an extra one."

So his phone was in there and his lifejacket was missing? She bit her bottom lip and turned away from him, scanning the creek bank, looking for any sign of Joe. If he'd fallen overboard, she really hoped that at least he had his lifejacket on. She knew Joe could swim but still, if something happened and...

She didn't want to let her mind go down that path. Life could be changed in a split second, something she knew well. She carried the scars to prove it.

But she didn't want any more pain for Mac's family, no more loss. They'd already lost their parents. It just seemed so damn unfair to lose more.

She continued scanning as he drove, the silence not awkward, more companionable than anything—except for the dark cloud hanging over their heads.

At the sound of a cell phone ringing, cutting through the quiet morning air, she shifted against her seat.

Mac answered. "Yeah?"

She sat there waiting, trying to read his expression as he listened to whoever was talking. Then she turned away, not wanting to miss anything onshore. The water was low compared to what she was used to in the afternoons, the tree roots visible and extending like long, spindly fingers into the water.

"No, his is blue and green," Mac said to whoever was on the other line. After a few more grunts, he hung up.

She looked at him expectantly.

"They found an old lifejacket on a tucked-away beach, but it's not his."

She didn't respond because she wasn't sure what to say, so she kept looking.

As the creek opened up into the river, she continued scanning, looking for *anything* that didn't belong.

For the next twenty minutes they were silent, both of them searching in vain, it felt like. The waterways around Verona Bay were vast—she'd looked at a map on

Google Earth last night and seeing it from an aerial view had been overwhelming. The blue lines had been fat and slender in places, covering a wide swath around the entire region.

"There!" Her heart jumped into her chest as she spotted a pop of color against brown. "I can't tell what it is." She stood, leaning forward as she tried to make sense of the bright turquoise tucked against a tree root.

Mac increased the speed as she leaned over even more. Blood rushed in her ears as she squinted against the rising sun glittering off the surface. Maybe it was just a beer can or—

Oh God, a sneaker. And it was Joe's. She recognized the distinctive turquoise and yellow combination.

Mac must have seen it too, because he cursed as he angled them toward the roots, pushing his boat through as far as he could. The trolling motor revved up water, but the boat was stuck on something.

He was trying to free it but it was taking too much time. Without thinking, she tugged off her shoes and jumped off the front of the boat. Cold water slapped her in the face, soaking through her clothes as she submerged.

"Adeline!"

"It's not deep!" Her feet brushed the bottom as she hurried forward, half-swimming, half-walking over the sand.

She heard him curse behind her, then heard the breaking of branches as she got closer.

Her heart rate stuttered when she saw the outline of Joe's jeans.

He was on his back, floating in a very shallow marshy area by the creek's riverbed, almost completely hidden from sight. "He's here! No, no, no," she muttered to herself as she splashed forward, scrambling through the water. Everything seemed to happen in slow motion, the water like sandbags holding her back as she tried to hurry faster, faster. As she reached his body, there was a splash behind her as she crouched down in the mud and muck. His lifejacket was hooked onto a twisted root and he had a bloody gash on his forehead. His skin was pale with a bluish tint. Oh, God.

Joe...

She tested his pulse as Mac slammed down into the water next to her, sending out waves in all directions. "He's alive," she said quickly, relief swamping her. "His pulse is faint and thready."

Wordlessly, Mac lifted Joe into his arms, ripping the lifejacket free from the root in a split second.

She hurried behind him, wading back through the brackish water to reach the idling boat. Her heart was a wild beat against her chest as she climbed over the side.

"I need to get him warm and check him for more wounds." Mac shoved his phone at her as he pulled out a Mylar blanket. His expression was tight, his movements economic. The weather wasn't unnaturally cold, but the creek water Joe had been in, had been chilled, likely from a natural spring. And there was no telling how long he'd been floating in it.

130 | KATIE REUS

Adeline took it, seeing he'd already dialed Lincoln. She quickly told the sheriff that they'd found Joe then set the phone down and put it on speaker so he could talk to Mac. She started tugging off Joe's soaked sneakers, helping Mac undress him down to his boxers. His skin was so damn pale, the blue of his veins visible.

"We won't be long," Mac said quickly to Lincoln. His expression was so tight, but she could see the emotions in his eyes, how worried he was for his brother. "Joe doesn't seem to have any breathing obstruction, but I'm bringing his core temperature up first. I'll be coming in fast so make sure the ambulance is ready."

"We're ready now," Lincoln said. "I'll radio everyone and tell them to stay put so no one gets in your way."

As soon as they had Joe wrapped in the blanket, she said, "I'll start cleaning his wound. You drive." She didn't know much about boats and he could get them there faster.

Nodding, he jumped in the back as she sat in the foot-well, holding Joe's head in her lap as Mac quickly steered out of the underbrush. She gently ran her fingers over Joe's pale forehead. His chest rose and fell in shallow bursts and while his body was chilled, his head felt incredibly hot. But at least he was breathing and getting warm now. She just prayed he made it.

Mac handed her the first-aid kit as he maneuvered down the creek as fast as possible. Little waves splayed out on either side of them as she opened the kit. There wasn't much she could do, but she managed to clean off the wound on his forehead with alcohol wipes and get rid of most of the dried blood. An ugly bruise had formed, his forehead a yellowish green. Since he wasn't bleeding, she didn't put a bandage on it because they'd be back at the marina soon and the EMTs would take over.

He'd gunned the engine so that they were flying over the water. As they sped forward, Mac called out over the sound of the wind rolling past them. "Here, take this." There were "no wake" signs but who gave a crap about that now.

She grabbed the T-shirt from him with a murmur of thanks. Without jostling Joe, she quickly took off the lifejacket and her own soaked shirt. She had spare pants in her pack, but she'd worry about that later. Keeping her back to Mac, she stripped the sopping shirt off and tossed it into the footwell in front of them.

She froze as she remembered what her back looked like.

Hell. Her scars.

Some days she completely forgot about them—like today. Wordlessly, she tugged the shirt on over her head and hoped Mac hadn't noticed.

Joe let out a soft moaning sound as she shifted his head against her lap. That had to be a good sign, right? He'd been so damn quiet, but sound and movement was good. "You're going to be okay," she murmured to him, hoping he could somehow hear her.

God, please let him be okay, she silently shouted. *Let today have a happy ending.* The world certainly needed more of them.

CHAPTER SEVENTEEN

Ezra looked at the message, a smile spreading across his face. Maybe his investment was going to pay off after all.

The message was simple. *I'm still interested in information.*

Ezra wrote back immediately. *I've found what you're looking for.* Technically he was waiting on a final confirmation that it was the right woman, but he was going with his gut on this. It had never steered him wrong. And if it ended up not being her? He'd just refund the guy. He wasn't going to rip anyone off. It was bad for business.

Barely five minutes later he received another message. *I want the information. I can wire your fee.*

Smiling to himself, he quickly typed back. *The fee has doubled.* It had been ten years, and while it hadn't taken a ton of work to find this target, he knew he was the only one looking for this woman. No one else on the forum had opened the offer in nearly eight years.

That's bullshit!

No, that's business. *I'm the only one with the information. This was a dead case and it took a lot of work. Take it or leave it.*

Twenty minutes trickled by as he worked on other projects.

Fine. I'll wire you half now and the other half once I've verified the information is good.

He could live with that. *No problem. If you try to double-cross me, I know who you are and I know where you live.* Then he sent an aerial shot of the man's house, not caring if he pissed him off or not. This guy might have had political connections at one time—and Ezra knew that he still had some—but he was a typical rich asshole. One who'd been born into wealth, not truly earned it. He had to hire people like Ezra to do his dirty work.

You'll have your money by the end of the day.

Ezra typed, *Do you need help taking care of the target? I have someone on retainer who is in pest control.* If the man didn't understand what pest control meant, then he was a moron—and this guy was definitely not stupid. He was rich as hell and had only gotten richer over the last ten years. Of course, it was on the backs of poor people, but no surprise. Men like him were all the same. Which was why Ezra didn't feel an ounce of guilt at charging him double. It was simply business.

I want the information only. I have someone who can handle things.

As soon as I have my money, you'll get all the information you need.

He logged off, not surprised it would take a few hours for the guy to send the money. It was a healthy chunk of change. And Ezra would be true to his word; as soon as he got paid, he would send the man all the information he would need to find the woman formerly known as Ana Diaz.

He glanced at his watch, then texted Tony. *Get me the final pictures and her new name.*

Tony replied almost immediately. *On it.*

He broke his burner phone apart, then grabbed his regular cell and scrolled to the number of the collector he'd bought his last car from. It was time to buy another toy.

CHAPTER EIGHTEEN

Autumn was barely paying attention as she hurried across the parking lot. Both Lincoln and Adeline had texted her that Joe had been found—alive, thankfully—and was at the hospital. She wished she could have left school earlier, but she'd forgotten about a couple parent-teacher conferences today, both of which had ended up being ridiculous. A couple emails could have covered the "issues".

So now she was on her way to pick up Adeline, who'd left her vehicle at the marina since her friend had rode to the hospital with Mac Collins.

"Ms. Perez?" An angry male voice drew her attention as she nearly reached her car.

Startled, she turned to find a man getting out of a big Chevy truck. He left the driver's side door open, the engine still running. She guessed that his hair had once been a dark brown, but it was liberally peppered with gray throughout. In jeans, sturdy boots and a faded T-shirt, he stalked toward her, his shoes making thumping sounds against the pavement.

"Can I help you?" Instinctively she held her teacher's bag in front of her and slid her hand into her purse to grab her pepper spray. As her fingers wrapped around it, some of her tension eased.

The older man's eyebrows were drawn together and his mouth was pinched into a tight line. And he was big too, looked as if he might have once played football or some kind of sport.

"My son, Mark Cadman, is in your class. He's a senior—and it's your fault that he's not getting to play in next Friday's game!"

She recognized the name immediately because Mark hadn't been turning in any of his assignments. "I have no idea what you're talking about. I have no control over football or basketball or whatever." She knew it took an incredible amount of discipline for kids to participate in sports, but she wasn't sure what Mark played because he didn't wear any sort of sports paraphernalia to indicate.

He took a menacing step toward her. "It's football, and because you're failing him, now he can't play!"

Autumn stood her ground. "I think what you mean to say is that because he's not turning in his assignments, he's failing. He is literally failing himself because he won't do the work. It's art class," she added, giving him a hard look. She hated being confronted by such a big guy but she wasn't backing down. She'd learned that with bullies, sometimes that was the best thing to do. And it was very clear that this guy was a bully. Because any man who would confront a woman alone in a nearly deserted parking lot like this? Yeah, he was definitely trying to intimidate her.

"He's too busy for art," he snapped.

"Then he needs to take another elective class. I'm not going to give him good grades for doing nothing. How hard do you think my class is?" The question was more or less rhetorical. "And if you would like to schedule a conference, I would be more than happy to do that—and to include the principal. Do *not* bother me in the school parking lot like this again. I don't respond well to bullies."

He actually looked shocked at her words—even as he took another menacing step toward her. "Bully?"

Desperate for a distraction, she pressed her car alarm on her key fob. It was either that or pepper spray him, because he had a dark look in his eyes that had her teeth on edge.

He looked around, startled, so she took the advantage and hurried toward her car, sliding inside and turning off the alarm as she locked the doors. "Asshole," she muttered.

He slammed his fist on the hood of her car, so she laid on the horn and looked him dead in the eye.

He jumped back as she kicked her car into drive and tore out of the parking lot. As one last parting shot, he slammed his fist on the hood as she shot past him. She looked in the rearview mirror and saw that he was hurrying to his truck.

Heart racing, hands trembling, she used the vehicle's OnStar system and called the principal.

Thankfully, Sheila picked up immediately. "Hey Autumn. Everything okay?"

"Mark Cadman's father just stopped me in the parking lot. He pounded on the front of my car and hood when I drove away from him. He's angry that Mark is getting a failing grade. I don't know what he would have done but... he scared me."

To her surprise, Sheila let out a fairly savage curse. She hadn't even realized the woman was capable of cursing. "He's not even supposed to be at the school," she said. "Mark lives with his mother because of custody issues. I think the dad was abusive. I'm going to alert the police right now. Are you okay? Do you need anything?"

Still shaking as she hurried down the road, she shook her head then realized she needed to answer audibly. "No, I'm okay. I just... I don't want to see him again."

When she looked in the rearview mirror, no one was behind her.

"You won't, don't worry. I will handle this *right* now."

"Thanks, you're the best." She'd gotten lucky that Verona Bay High was such a good school—and Sheila's leadership was part of the reason why she was hesitant to accept the offer at the cultural center. A principal could make or break a school, and Sheila was a true leader who cared about both her teachers and her students.

She glanced in the rearview mirror as she turned onto the two-lane backroad highway. The hospital was technically in the next town, but it was more or less on the outskirts of Verona Bay. And there was only one way to get there. Thankfully it would only take twenty minutes, but she wished she was there right now.

She knew it was unlikely that the man would follow her, but she couldn't help the feeling that someone was watching her. She thought about calling Lincoln, but didn't want to bug him when she knew Sheila was already taking care of things. She couldn't run to him for everything, especially because she knew he was the type of man to drop everything for her now that they were having a baby together. No, she couldn't abuse their relationship like that.

"Stupid paranoia," she muttered to herself as a jacked-up Jeep zoomed around her. The rumble of the tires were loud and obnoxious, but she managed to shake off most of the residual tension in her shoulders after about ten minutes of driving and listening to soothing music.

Pop!

She let out a yelp as her car jerked to the right. Gripping the wheel hard, she tried to keep control as the car fishtailed, swerving back and forth across the two lanes.

Her heart leapt into her throat as she struggled to gain control, to slow down as it shook and shuddered from the blown tire.

Instead of slamming on the brakes, she shifted to neutral and eased her foot on down, barely holding on to control as she slid onto the grassy patch on the side of the road. As her car finally stopped, she couldn't stop the wild beat of her heart.

Blood rushed in her ears as she took stock of herself. There were no cars coming in the other direction and none in the rearview mirror.

Still feeling jittery, she grabbed her pepper spray and eased out of her vehicle. The back of her neck prickled and she could swear someone was watching her. The thought was ridiculous—she was in the middle of nowhere.

The faint scent of smoke lingered in the air from a controlled fire a few weeks back. The huge pine trees on either side of the road had been thinned out, parts of the underbrush brown and sooty. It was so quiet, she felt like the only person in the world right now.

If someone was here, she would know, right? Still, she couldn't shake the uneasy sensation of fingers crawling up her back even as she walked to the rear of her car, her pepper spray gripped tightly in her fingers. She winced. The rubber on the back tire had a huge hole in it, the thing completely flat. She'd gotten flats before, but this… she must have hit a nail or something huge. There was no way she'd be able to patch this thing up either.

Cursing, she popped her trunk, glad she had a spare.

She had AAA, but she wasn't sure how long they would take and even though she absolutely hated changing tires, she could do it quicker than the time it would take someone to get here. Still, what if Mark Cadman's father came after her and found her on this deserted road?

She started to call AAA, but at the sound of an engine revving, she listened to her fight-or-flight instinct and hurried around the side of her car, the thick blades of grass brushing over her feet and around her ankles. She crouched down behind her car to give her cover as a huge truck pulled to a stop behind her.

She clutched her only weapon as the front door opened, heart thudding.

She froze when she saw a woman named Clarice get out. Autumn didn't know her well, just knew that she had a thick country accent and was at the local diner a lot.

She hurried around from behind her car and nodded politely at the other woman.

"Car trouble?" the woman asked, stating the obvious as she eyed the tire. Her blonde hair was big, her huge hoop earring glittering as they caught the fading sunlight.

"Yeah, I don't know what happened." She strode to the back, frowning down at the mess.

Clarice let out a low whistle. "You must have hit a nail or bunch of them. That almost looks like someone shot out your tire," she drawled with a shake of her head.

Her panic must've shown on her face because Clarice just laughed. "I'm kidding. I can't imagine someone shooting at ya. You're the art teacher at the cultural center, right? You teach all those classes?"

Autumn nodded, even as a thread of unease wound down her spine. Somehow she found a real smile. "I am. My name's Autumn."

"I'm Clarice." Setting bright pink nails on her jean-clad hips, she smiled. "I can help you change your tire if you want?"

She blinked. "Yeah that would be great, thank you so much."

Twenty minutes later, she was incredibly grateful to the woman. It would've been a hell of a lot harder to do it by herself on the side of the road as she worried about passing vehicles. And the truth was, Autumn wasn't sure she actually could have done it by herself on this partial incline. Not to mention she was still rattled from her encounter at the school.

Once Clarice was done, she offered her money, not even sure how much something like this would cost.

"I'm not taking your money." Clarice wiped her hands on a towel she'd grabbed from her truck as she declined Autumn's offer. "Maybe you give me a discount on one your classes?"

"You can take one for free. Seriously, thank you so much for this."

"Heck, yeah. Women need to help each other."

Autumn found herself smiling again. "Amen to that."

With her ruined tire in the trunk, she made a mental note to take it by the auto body shop so they could tell her what happened. She needed to get a new spare now anyway.

She also needed to tell Lincoln. Even if Sheila had already called the sheriff's department, she wanted to tell him about this too.

* * *

Autumn stepped into the hospital waiting room, immediately scanning for Adeline.

"Hey, thank you so much for coming," Adeline said to Autumn as she jumped up from her seat in the hospital waiting room.

The place was fairly packed, with about seventy-five percent of the seats taken and a cluster of people standing in line at the free coffee stand in the corner. The walls were a pale gray, the floors a shiny white and the cushy chairs a mint green. A low hum of voices filled the room, but mostly everyone was keeping to themselves.

Autumn hurried forward, taking in her friend in a quick visual sweep. Adeline had on scrub bottoms and a shirt that was far too big for her tall, slender frame. "So what did they say?"

"I think he's going to be okay. He'd been unconscious for a while. It looks like his boat got away from him when he was leaning over to grab some trash. He fell out, hit his head, and I think he might have been drinking a little. I'm not really sure on the particulars yet. But his brothers are in with him and he's actually spoken a few times and seems to make sense."

"That's great..." Autumn glanced over as Mac Collins strode out, his flannel shirt shoved up to his elbows and circles under his eyes.

Immediately, he zeroed in on Adeline.

They both turned to him as he hurried forward and, to Autumn's surprise, pulled Adeline into a big hug.

Adeline seemed startled but hugged him back, laughing a little awkwardly. "I hope that means everything is definitely okay?" she asked as he set her back on her feet.

"He's going to be okay. A little banged up and I think embarrassed that everyone was out looking for him. But it's a good thing we were, or he..." He swallowed hard and rubbed a hand over his dark hair as he looked at Adeline. "Anyway, I really just wanted to say thank you again."

"Of course. Did you need anything while I'm still here?"

"I'm good. Dylan's already gone down to grab us food from the cafeteria. We're both going to stay the night if they'll let us. Thanks though."

Adeline looked as if she might respond, then a doctor waved Mac over. He said a quick goodbye before hurrying off.

"You want to hang out for a while?" Autumn asked. "The hospital cafeteria food is actually pretty good here."

"No, he's okay, and that's all I really needed to know."

"Are you sure?"

Adeline picked up her backpack. "Yeah. It's not like I'm family or anything. I'm just his tutor."

Autumn fell into step with her friend as they headed into the hallway. "Serenity said that you rode in Mac's boat today. Kinda seems like you're more than just a tutor. Is he who you've been dating?"

Adeline shot her a sideways glance. "I actually haven't been dating anyone," she murmured. "I've been doing a lot of tutoring lately. Just to save money—I'm hoping to buy a house next year. And... I have a bit of a crush on Mac, which is probably obvious to everyone. Every time I think about that man, I swear my cheeks heat up."

"I didn't know, I swear." Adeline was so good at masking her emotions.

"Really?"

"I promise. Look, have you eaten at all today?"

She shook her head. "I had some coffee and a muffin this morning. But I haven't left the waiting room since we rushed here. Mac asked me to hang out for a while and I didn't want him to think I'd left."

As they stepped through the sliding exit doors, Autumn was surprised by the cool breeze. There was a shift in the air, telling her that fall was starting to creep in. Not that Florida had a real fall season, but at least it wasn't as sweltering as August.

A big man moved past them, nearly knocking her down. He gave her a hard look, almost as if he was surprised to see her. But that made no sense—she didn't know him.

"Excuse me," she murmured, frowning at him.

He gave her a strange look, or maybe that was her imagination. After the day she'd had, she was simply on edge—and in need of some kind of sustenance. Her little peanut wasn't happy she hadn't eaten since lunch. She was borderline nauseous at this point.

"This way," she said to Adeline. "I parked across the street. And I'm going to take you downtown so we can get some pie—or we can do a drive-through so you can get easy food. It looks like you might need a shower. Did you jump in the water?" Adeline hadn't said much in her texts.

She nodded slightly, looking exhausted. "Yeah, it was... terrifying. I thought he was dead," she whispered.

"I didn't realize you guys were the ones who found him."

She shoved out a breath as they reached Autumn's car, parked under one of the huge lights. "I saw his shoe and recognized it. I didn't think, just jumped in. But when I got to him…" She shook her head.

"All right, you are *definitely* getting some pie tonight."

"Are you sure?" Adeline asked as she slid into the passenger seat and lay her head back against the headrest. "I know you've got a class at the cultural center in the morning."

"It's fine. It's only seven o'clock. We're not eighty." As she pulled out of the parking lot, Autumn felt those eyes on her again and cursed herself for the fear welling up inside her. She hated that it affected her life, her moods, and tried to shove it back down into that little box in her head. She wished she could see Lincoln right now—or go home to him. Which was a ludicrous thought, but there it was. She wondered far too often what it would be like to have him come home to her every night or vice versa.

Adeline snorted. "Speak for yourself. I love being home and in bed by eight."

Autumn rolled her eyes as she took a left turn. "You're ridiculous."

"Maybe so. And I'm pretty sure I'm going to eat pie and only pie for dinner tonight. Maybe I'll eat a whole one."

"I would say you've earned it."

CHAPTER NINETEEN

When she spotted a familiar vehicle in her driveway, Autumn automatically tensed, her shoulders bunching up. Talking with Adeline had been cathartic and she was so damn relieved that Joe was okay. But at the sight of the vehicle in her driveway, she didn't think she had the mental energy to deal with another blow today. This entire day felt like it had been a decade. Her classes, that confrontation in the school parking lot, her tire blowing out so violently. She was flat out done at this point. At least it was Friday, the only silver lining right now.

She pulled in next to Erica, glad it was her handler and not Erica's partner. Not that she didn't like Derek, but Erica had been with her from the beginning.

By the time she got out of her car, purse in hand, Erica was out as well. In khakis, a blue polo shirt, and sneakers, she looked the same as she always did. Her short hair was pulled up into a tiny ponytail—Autumn knew she kept it just long enough so she could pull it off her face.

"I tried calling," Erica said.

"I've been at the hospital—just picking up a friend. I had my phone off and," she glanced in her purse, "I never turned the volume back up. Sorry."

Erica lifted an eyebrow. "You don't sound sorry."

"I already told you guys, I'm not moving." She really tried to keep the attitude out of her voice, but wasn't sure she succeeded.

Erica held up a hand. "I know. I just wanted to talk to you, and we need to have this conversation in person."

She couldn't read Erica's expression, had never been able to really. The woman was damn good at her job— she'd been good at convincing Autumn to join WITSEC and she'd always kept tabs on her. Even after the so-called danger zone time had passed. Technically the danger would never be gone. Not while Rand Coventry was alive.

Once they were inside and she'd disarmed her security system, she pointed at the kitchen as she petted Shadow with her other hand. "You want a drink? Or do you want to do this in the living room?"

"Water would be good. I've been drinking crap coffee the last few hours."

As she headed down the hallway, Shadow stuck to her, dancing around her ankles and soaking up being petted, barely looking at Erica. She must have decided that the other woman wasn't a threat or of interest to her.

"Who's this little lady?" Erica asked as Autumn opened the back door to let Shadow out to do her business.

"You didn't come to talk about my dog." Okay, she knew she sounded like a bitch at this point, but she didn't care. It had been a long day and if Erica was going to try convince her to move, they were going to have it out right now.

"You're freaking cranky," Erica murmured as she sat at the center island. "For the record, I'm not here to tell you to move," she added.

"You probably should have led with that." She slid an ice-cold bottle of water in front of Erica. "Are you hungry? I can rustle up some snacks." Now that she knew her handler wasn't here to harass her about moving, she was feeling a little better.

Erica's mouth curved up slightly. "I'm good, thank you."

A few moments later, Shadow ran back inside and Autumn shut the door behind her dog, locking it automatically.

After filling up Shadow's bowls with food and water, she sat across the island from Erica. "Well?"

"Rand Coventry was killed in a prison transport. We're still not sure what happened, the guards were killed, and so was the other prisoner they were transporting."

"What? He's *dead*? Are you sure?" Questions fired out of her one after the other as she tried to wrap her mind around this huge news. Something inside her snapped free in that moment, a pressure she hadn't even known was there. It was as if she could breathe a little better.

"We've got a positive ID on his dental records, but we're testing the DNA to be sure. Still, it looks as if it's him."

She frowned. "Wait, why do they need to test the DNA?"

Erica wrapped her fingers around the bottle but didn't open it. Her fingernails were short and neat with no polish. She never wore any makeup either.

She watched Autumn with bright blue eyes for a long moment. "We're actually investigating the crash. It looks like they were forced off the road, maybe in a botched breakout attempt. The passenger with Coventry was the younger brother of a high-level... Well, I can't technically say, but his brother is involved with the drug trade. And the bullets that busted up the grill and engine block are used with a very specific type of weapon his brother's people have been known to use. From what we've gathered, the rescue went sour when the vehicle suddenly caught fire. A freak accident, it looks like. The bodies are mostly burned beyond recognition so we're testing DNA to cross all our t's and dot all our i's. But the dental records for both men line up with what we have so the DNA is a formality at this point."

"What about the guys who tried to help him escape?"

"They managed to evade the local cops. It happened in a desolate area where law enforcement is stretched thin." Erica gritted her teeth, clearly annoyed with that.

"So... What does this mean for me?" A roller coaster of emotions swept through her. She wiped damp palms on her dress as her body went clammy. Could he really be dead after all this time? She was almost too afraid to hope for it.

"It could mean any number of things. If you want to go back to being Ana Diaz—only once it's confirmed that Coventry is truly dead—there's a slim chance you can. Or you can remain Autumn Perez. We still don't know if his family was involved in putting that hit out on you ten years ago. Personally I don't think he was smart enough to have done it himself—I hate that I could never prove it, but I think his father was behind it. He had the money and the connections. All that said, I think you should stay in the program."

Autumn nodded slowly as another band around her chest snapped free. Even if Rand's father had been involved, Rand himself had always been a threat in her mind. It felt kind of morbid to be glad that the threat was gone, but she couldn't control her internal reaction.

Next to her, Shadow whined softly so she reached out and petted her head, stroking her soft fur. "Ana Diaz died a long time ago." She'd made peace with that fact years ago, she'd had to in order to survive. She wasn't that woman anymore. "I like where I live. And… I'm pregnant." With a man who made her feel far too many things, made her *want* too many things.

Erica's eyes widened in true surprise, probably the first time Autumn had ever surprised her.

She gave her handler a ghost of a smile. "Yeah, that's about how I felt when I found out too. The father and I are… friends. I'm not leaving. I didn't tell Derek because frankly it's none of his business, but that's why you need to understand that no matter what happens, I will never leave here. The father's whole family is here, and I would never ask him to join WITSEC." And she didn't want that life for her child either.

A long pause stretched between them before Erica let out a low whistle. "Okay then. Noted. Look, nothing's really changed. Not on your end, anyway. And if you're not leaving the program, then just keep living your life the way you always have. With the exception of the one mistake you made, you've been an absolute model participant. I wish everyone treated the program like you did."

Autumn wished that people didn't have to go in the program at all, but that wasn't how life worked. "When will you know if it was him? I mean, I'm not leaving the program anyway but... I still want to know."

"Forty-eight hours maybe. It's in the lab, but it's not a priority given how old his case is. I'll let you know as soon as I do. You'll be my first phone call, I promise."

"Thank you."

"Oh, I've got this for you." She slid an envelope across the countertop.

Autumn recognized Hector's bold handwriting and smiled. They'd kept in touch over the years, through Erica and the US Marshals. They were allowed to actually mail each other letters, but the marshals acted as a go-between—and they read every single correspondence. Hector was the only person she'd stayed in touch with after everything. In a way it sucked, because she couldn't be fully honest about her life, couldn't give too many details just in case. But he kept her apprised of her old neighborhood, of how his studio was doing, his life in

general, and it helped her stay tethered to that other
world. She was glad for it, even if she wasn't Ana anymore. That was the first chapter of her life, or at least
that was how she looked at it. And she liked holding on
to the connection to that chapter even if it was closed.

Autumn stepped out onto the porch with Erica, a mix
of emotions pummeling her as she watched the other
woman leave. The bright lights of Lincoln's truck flashed
as he pulled into his driveway.

Making a split-second decision, she crossed her yard
to meet him.

She was going to tell him the truth. Tell him about
her past. It was pretty doubtful that Rand Coventry had
managed to fake his own death—why wait so long? And
even if he had, she was staying here, and she wanted Lincoln to know the truth about her. All of her. Hopefully it
would also explain why she couldn't be with him.

He pulled into his garage but instead of closing it, he
strode out, his expression exhausted. "Hey, Autumn."

"How are you?" she asked.

"Tired," he said with a wan smile. "But Joe is going to
be okay. He was damn lucky he's got a big brother who
was so damn worried about him. If we'd been even a little later getting that search party set up..." He shook his
head.

As she watched him, she thought about what a truly
good man he was, inside and out. For a moment, she
wondered if she should tell him any of this, but... he deserved to know. "Do you have a few minutes to talk
about something important? Well, maybe more than a

few minutes? If you're too tired, we can talk tomorrow though." Yeah, she probably should have waited.

"Yeah. Let me take off my duty belt and change. I can be over in a few minutes?"

She nodded. "I'll leave the front door unlocked. I was about to heat up some leftover Chinese food. Are you hungry?"

"Nah. I grabbed dinner from Momma's Kitchen."

"Okay, I'll see you in a few." Her heart raced as she tried to think of the best way to tell him.

She'd dropped a whole lot on him in the span of only a couple days. She had to give Lincoln credit, he was taking the whole pregnancy thing in stride, and in a way that she didn't think most men would. She'd had a friend back in college who'd gotten pregnant and the father had completely wiped his hands of all responsibility, saying that he would pay child support but the kid wasn't his problem. She didn't understand attitudes like that, but unfortunately they were all too common. Which was why she'd been prepping for Lincoln to want nothing to do with her after her news.

He took longer than she'd expected, which ended up being a good thing because she had time to eat. And she'd discovered that she needed to eat fairly regularly or she got nauseous. Supposedly it was normal for the first trimester, and she was grateful that she hadn't had any morning sickness yet. But she also knew that she wasn't out of the woods.

As she was washing her dish, she heard the front door open and Lincoln call out. "It's just me!"

Shadow perked up, her tail wagging as she looked up at Autumn.

Autumn shook her head down at the adorable collie. "I really think you're part cat. What if that had been a robber?" she murmured, only to be licked on her calf before Shadow went down on her front paws and lolled her head to the side, watching her.

As Lincoln strode into the room, she dried her hands on the dishtowel and tried not to stare at him too hard. He was just so damn gorgeous. His hair was damp and he had on jeans and a T-shirt that molded to a hard chest and abs, leaving little to her imagination—and she didn't have to imagine, since she'd kissed every inch of that chest. Ugh. Maybe part of being pregnant also meant being super horny. Every time she saw Lincoln, she wanted a repeat of what had led to said pregnancy.

"Sorry I took a little longer," he said as he crouched down to greet Shadow.

For her part, Shadow jumped on him, licking his face excitedly. Shameless.

"No problem. I know you've had a long day so I appreciate you coming over. I have something big to tell you and there's really no easy way to do it." She motioned to the island countertop.

"You can tell me anything," he said quietly as he sat across from her, watching her in that intense way of his that guaranteed she got all his focus.

It was kind of unnerving because she knew he was really, truly listening. "You want anything to drink?"

He shook his head, all his focus on her.

She shoved out a breath. Maybe it was a mistake to tell him, but screw it; she didn't care what the marshals thought. She wasn't going to tell Erica what she was doing anyway. She wasn't a young woman alone in a new city who was scared of starting over and panicking by telling a fool she'd thought she loved. She was telling a man she trusted, the father of her child.

"When I was twenty-two, I saw a man named Rand Coventry dumping the dead body of a woman behind an art studio I worked at."

His eyes widened in surprise but he remained quiet, letting her talk.

She was glad he was so patient as she tried to work through everything, to get it all out at once so she wouldn't have to talk about this again. "I won't go into *all* the details now but I was a witness to the dumping of her murdered body, and I managed to get some pictures of him. Though I wasn't trying to get evidence or anything, I was terrified. I was taking the pictures in order to blind him with my flash so I could get away.

"Once the cops had his picture, it didn't take long for them to figure out who he was. It went to trial and he was convicted for her rape and murder. During the trial, someone tried to kill me—twice. Once, my brake lines were cut. And another time a masked man with a gun broke into my apartment. I got away just barely and the DA put me in protective custody. After the trial, they thought it best if I went into witness protection. I weighed my options and decided to do it. It was... difficult. My given name is not Autumn Perez. It's Ana Diaz."

He watched her, his eyes dilating slightly, but he was still silent.

"Did you have any questions?"

"You're very brave," he said in a soothing voice.

That wasn't a question, but it made her smile. "I certainly don't feel like it. The trial was... hard." That being an understatement. "I was what the district attorney considered a 'perfect witness' if that makes sense."

"I do, unfortunately. A lot of times witnesses or victims are treated as criminals, especially in cases involving rape. It's disgusting."

She shoved out a breath, glad he understood. "Apparently I did well under cross-examination. To be honest, I don't remember all of it. I just tried to stay calm and answer questions factually. I saw what I saw and I reported that. I didn't know who Coventry was, didn't go to school with him so I had no axe to grind. It also helped that I was a scholarship kid who'd gotten a degree based on hard work and merit, and he was painted by the media as a rich kid whose father had bailed him out of tons of scrapes during college—including sexual assault accusations. That's all true—it turned out he'd gotten into some trouble with the law but it had all been brushed under the rug. But my testimony is what really cinched things. I saw him dumping the body and he came after me. He never hurt me, but it's pretty damn clear he hadn't wanted to simply talk to me when he broke into the studio where I was hiding. So his statement that she'd died of an overdose and he panicked and dumped her might have gotten him less time, but the fact that he came after me is, what I think, swayed them to go after him *hard*. Plus his father was well known in the area so they couldn't afford to look soft on crime."

"Jesus," he murmured. "You're incredible."

She cleared her throat. "Since going into WITSEC, I've moved around a couple times but I'm not moving again. The person you saw leaving when you got home not too long ago is my handler with the program. She just let me know that Coventry is very likely dead—killed in a prison transport." There was no reason not to tell Lincoln the details when he could easily search for them at this point. "She's not totally sure, but the marshals seem to think there's a good chance he is. Something happened and it looks like he was killed as collateral damage. I don't have that many details but the fact that she showed up here in person tells me she believes he's dead. They've got a match with the dental records, but they're waiting on a DNA match to confirm."

"Is she trying to move you or let you out of the program?"

She blinked at his question, but of course he would know more about WITSEC than a civilian. He was a cop after all and probably dealt with the marshals occasionally. "She thinks I should stay in the program regardless. I never thought Rand was smart enough to have sent someone to kill me. If I had to guess, his father was behind everything. He was a state senator back then."

Lincoln frowned slightly. "I don't recognize the name."

"You wouldn't. It was in California, and his political career died a savage death after what his son did. It was a very long, drawn-out case, and after his son was found guilty, he had no chance of ever getting reelected for anything again. Honestly, even if his son had been let off, I don't know that he would have been reelected regardless. He went into some kind of finance career. I have no idea what he does exactly, I certainly didn't keep tabs on him."

"That's incredible. *You're* incredible," he added. "Thank you for telling me."

He always knew the right thing to say, exactly how to make her feel stronger than she actually was. "After today, I felt like I needed to. I'll never go back to being Ana, that girl died a long time ago. And I think this goes without saying, but what I've told you stays between us." She couldn't control if he told someone, but... she trusted him in a way she didn't trust most people. "You can't even tell your family."

He nodded. "I would never."

The tension bands around her chest eased even more. "Since I'm being so honest, I'm going to tell you more about my past. If you want to hear it? I've dropped so much on you the last couple days, so if you've met your quota for drama, I understand."

He frowned at her. "It's not drama. Don't downplay this. It's your life, and yes, I want to know anything you're willing to share."

He really was incredible. She swallowed as she tried to get to this next part, to just rip off the rest of the band aid. "Going into the program wasn't easy, but it was made easier by the fact that I didn't have any blood family left. My mother was murdered, by her boyfriend at the time." She cleared her throat and glanced away as she drew a breath. It didn't matter that so much time had passed, the ache in her chest spread, pressing down on her as if a tiny elephant sat there. "He was a cop."

Lincoln sucked in a breath.

"She always had terrible taste in men. I have no idea who my father was, and I don't think she did either. She was a giving woman who simply wanted someone to love her and take care of her. She had such a big heart but she always seemed to find the losers—leeches who just sucked her dry of joy." Autumn reached down and petted Shadow, who was whining softly beside her. Shadow really was good at understanding the shifts in her moods. Just stroking her fingers through her fur was soothing. She would definitely give her sweet girl extra treats later. "So I just want you to understand that while I know you and I are having a baby together, we can never *be* together. I won't deny my attraction to you, but there are just too many complications for us to make any sense."

"Because of what happened to your mom?"

"Look, my mom was killed in violence, my whole *life* was taken because of violence, and you're a cop. I don't think you're anything like him—I wouldn't have slept with you or told you about my past if I did. You've shown me that time and again. But your job is dangerous, and you go out on bad calls more often than I'm sure I want to think about. I'm not going to lose someone else to violence." She simply couldn't take it.

"Anything could happen to me, even while driving home from work." His words were spoken calmly, logically.

And she knew them to be true. But her heart didn't care. "Maybe so, but that's how I feel." She wondered if she was lying to herself, throwing up reasons so she didn't have to open up her heart. Her life.

He watched her for a long moment, his eyes searching hers. "I appreciate you telling me all of this. Truly, I know this had to be a lot," he said as she heard his phone buzz in his pocket again.

It had gone off at least five times. "That's buzzed quite a lot. Do you need to get it?"

"No... damn it, yes," he said as he glanced at it, his jaw going tight.

"If you've got to work, I totally get it." And she did. She needed some time to mentally decompress after everything she'd just unloaded on him. She felt... free. Not completely, because fear always lingered in the back of her subconscious that Rand would find her, kill her.

But she'd been able to be honest with one person for the first time in ten years. It was definitely freeing, especially because it was Lincoln and she trusted him.

"Autumn, I hate to do this—"

"Go, I promise it's okay. I'm sort of drained after telling you all that anyway."

His body language was stiff as he stood, so she rounded the island and gave him an impulsive hug. He was going off on a call that she guessed was likely dangerous—or she didn't think he'd be leaving right now.

His embrace was tight, his whole body loosening from that awkward stance as he hugged her back. She leaned into him, burying her face against his chest—against her better judgement. He smelled so damn good and was so solid. He'd been so steady and wonderful.

"We're talking more about this later," he murmured against the top of her head, holding her longer than was necessary.

She didn't care, craved it even. Which flew in the face of everything she'd just told him, but being in his arms made it difficult to think clearly.

When he stepped back, he said, "Make sure you lock your door and set your alarm when I leave."

Maybe she should be a little annoyed at his brusque tone, but she knew he cared and it was clear he hated leaving. And okay, his protectiveness was sweet. He wanted her to be safe. It was foreign to have someone so invested in her. "I will, promise."

He paused, his big body vibrating with energy, but he eventually turned and hurried out.

As soon as he left—and she'd secured her house—she headed straight for bed. Today had been exhausting and now she felt as if she could sleep for an eternity.

She didn't even remember her head hitting the pillow.

Heart pounding, Autumn jerked up in bed at the sound of glass breaking—and her alarm piercing the air.

Shadow barked wildly, jumping to the floor, her tail sticking straight up.

Disoriented, blood rushing in her ears, Autumn rolled out of bed, reaching for her cell phone. This wasn't a dream.

My God, someone had broken into her house. She hurried to her bedroom door, shut and locked it with trembling fingers. It took two tries to dial 911 as she tugged Shadow with her to the bathroom. She did the same thing with this door, shutting it and locking it behind them. She tried to get her heart rate under control as the phone rang, but it was useless. All she could think was that he'd found her after all these years.

"911 operator, how may I help you?"

Hearing those familiar words brought back a flood of memories, but she managed to speak even over the blaring sound of her security alarm. "Someone has broken into my house. My alarm system is going off and I'm hiding in the bathroom." Her words sounded calm when inside she was screaming, desperate for help. She hoped the alarm had scared off the intruder—and that the cops got here fast.

She had to protect more than just herself now.

CHAPTER TWENTY

With his back against the wall by the rear door, Lincoln held up his fingers, indicating he and his deputy were going to storm the house.

Normally he negotiated with people, especially in any sort of domestic situation. He wanted everyone walking away from this unharmed, but Ryan Miller had been screaming obscenities at them for half an hour, refusing to come out or release his wife, June. At least he'd let his six-year-old daughter, Jennie, go.

That was a good sign—but June had screamed two minutes ago for a brief moment before the sound was abruptly cut off.

Two minutes felt like an eternity but it had taken them that long to surround the house and get into place at the back door. They weren't waiting any longer, and Miller wasn't responding to phone calls or the bullhorn.

Lincoln looked at his deputy, Andre Hill, then quickly picked the lock. Normally he'd kick a door in, but they wanted some element of surprise if possible. Two of his men were still out front using the bullhorn every fifteen seconds.

As he popped the door open, with Hill right behind him, they both swept inside, weapons up.

According to Jennie, her father had been keeping them cooped up in the main bedroom near the front of the house.

"I'm not leaving my house!" Miller screamed, presumably at Lincoln's guy who'd just used the bullhorn, his voice carrying from deeper in the house.

Lincoln followed it, sweeping the kitchen as he passed. The room was trashed, the small round table turned upside down, plates broken on the tile floor and splatters of blood on the white-washed cabinet by the sink.

They kept going, following more splatters of blood along the honey wood hallway.

Behind him, Hill was silent, and Lincoln had no doubt his deputy had his back. Hill had worked in Miami for a couple years and had been in the Army, so he was well-trained with weapons and knew how to remain calm in a volatile situation.

Instead of calling out, trying to negotiate again, Lincoln took a small, round mirror and eased it around the corner of the wall separating them from the hallway, trying to get a good view of what was going on without getting his head blown off. Small towns didn't have a SWAT team or the kind of equipment often found in larger cities, so he had to make do with what he had.

The bedroom door was three-quarters of the way open and Lincoln watched as Miller muttered to himself, pacing back and forth at the end of the bed, pistol in his hand. He hit the butt of the pistol against his own head as he made nonsensical sounds.

Lincoln could see June's dark hair splayed out on the floor near the foot of the bed. Her head was turned away and he couldn't tell if she was breathing or what kind of injury she had. But she wasn't moving. Damn it.

When Miller stepped out of sight, Lincoln motioned for Hill to follow. They hurried down the hall, weapons facing the open door. Adrenaline surging through him, he made it down the hallway in moments.

Together they burst into the bedroom. "Drop it now!" Lincoln shouted.

Miller jerked and turned, raising his pistol.

Lincoln fired, hitting him in the forearm. Miller's weapon clattered to the floor as he screamed.

"Check on the woman," he ordered his deputy as he raced at Miller, tackling him onto the bed.

Even though he'd been shot, Miller flailed at him, grazing his fist against Lincoln's temple.

He jerked back, grabbing Miller's arm and twisting him over onto his stomach.

As he did, he saw a flash of a blade before he felt it skim against his side—right below his vest.

Grunting, he elbowed Miller across the face before slamming him down against the bed and yanking his arms back, cuffing his wrists.

The guy cried out, writhing against the covers as the others rushed in.

"Shut the hell up," he growled as he jerked Miller to his feet and marched the now sobbing man outside. The guy was going on and on about how sorry he was. Too little too late, asshole.

Lincoln ignored him as one of the EMTs staunched the bleeding on Miller's arm—and the guy would *still* not shut the hell up. The EMT also gave Lincoln a bundle of gauze pads to stop his own bleeding so he shoved them under his shirt, wincing as they made contact with the slice.

He wasn't sure if June would make it, and though he hadn't confirmed it with Hill yet, he could tell she'd been stabbed at least once, given the amount of blood on the front of her shirt.

Hill rushed out with the other two EMTs who were rolling June across the front yard on a gurney.

"June!" Miller cried out, but Lincoln kept him firmly in place when he tried to get up and run to her.

"I told you to shut up." Lincoln turned the guy around so he couldn't even look at his wife. There were a few neighbors across the street watching, and even though they hadn't put up a barrier, no one was crossing over into the crime scene area.

"The other ambulance is on the way," one of his guys said to him. "They'll get him to the hospital."

As the ambulance tore off with June, its sirens blaring, Lincoln passed Miller off to one of his deputies and got a SITREP with Hill. June had been stabbed three times and they weren't sure if she was going to make it. Jennie had been taken back to the station so she wouldn't have to see any of this and would be meeting with a social worker. Thankfully, June had a sister who was going to take Jennie in for a while. Lincoln knew the sister, she was a good sort, so he was glad she'd be in a safe environment.

He hated this whole situation, but Miller wasn't getting out of it this time. In the past, June had refused to press charges—refused to admit that her husband had been abusing her at all. They'd had no way to prove it either if she wouldn't cooperate. Now he'd be charged with attempted murder.

When Lincoln heard the sound of the other ambulance approaching, he breathed out a sigh of relief. *Good.* He wanted to get Miller to the hospital, patched up, then processed. Because screw this guy. He could be sorry all he wanted—he'd terrorized his family and stabbed the woman he was supposed to love three times. There was a special place in hell for people like him.

"You bleeding, Sheriff?" Aaliyah asked as she jumped out of the passenger seat, frowning as she took in the blood trailing down onto his tan pants.

"It's just a nick."

Her frown grew. "We're going to need to look at that."

"I'm the one who's been shot!" Miller shouted.

"Take care of him first. I'm following you guys in my car."

It was clear she didn't like that, but she and her partner worked quickly and efficiently, not bothering to respond to Miller's ramblings as they got him into the back of the ambulance.

As Lincoln got into his cruiser, he lifted his shirt and peeled back the gauze. Two inches and still bleeding, but it was shallow. A great Friday night. At least it wasn't too bad, but he did need to get it patched up.

His adrenaline was dropping by the time he made it to the hospital. Instead of following them into the ER, he radioed Hill to stick with Miller. And even though he would have preferred to stay with Miller until he was fully processed, Lincoln knew he had to follow protocol. He'd been injured during an arrest, and acting like a jackass and refusing to get it taken care of wasn't a good look for the sheriff.

By the time he'd finished getting patched up, Hill strode into the room, his expression neutral. "Your neighbor, Autumn Perez, had a break-in at her house."

Stomach dropping, he jumped off the hospital bed, winced at the pull on the Steri-Strips. "Is she—"

"She's fine. Completely unharmed. Her alarm must have scared the guy off. The responding officer documented large boot footprints in her flower bed, but that's it."

That was too much. He needed to call her. "Who's with her?"

"Natalie."

She was one of his best detectives, had been working double duty tonight because they'd gotten so many callouts. "Good. What's going on with June?"

"Looks like she's gonna pull through. It's a miracle, he missed all major arteries. She lost a lot of blood but the doctors are very hopeful. The little girl is still with social services but her aunt is en route from Macon, should be here soon. She seems to be good people and has been trying to get June to leave that piece of crap for ages."

Lincoln scrubbed a hand over his face, fighting exhaustion. The poor girl had seen a whole lot tonight, and he just hoped that she wouldn't be scarred for life. He'd never understood how a parent could hurt their own child. The very thought was anathema to him. And tonight just drove home how much he wanted to keep Autumn and their peanut safe. "It must be a full moon tonight," he muttered.

Hill snorted. "No shit."

"I'll be out in a minute," he said as he pulled out his cell phone. Even though he wanted to call Autumn, he knew that if he heard her voice, he would rush right over there. Right now there was too much going on. But he wanted to text her at least, to know for certain she was okay.

Thankfully she texted him back moments later. *We're okay. Shadow was barking like crazy, ready to defend me.* Then she sent some cute emojis with smiley faces and puppies.

All the tension in his shoulders eased as he responded, though he was still concerned. Who the hell had tried to break in? *Stay safe... Do you want me to come over? I can be there if you need me.* Because screw procedure, he would rush right over there if she needed him.

Her response was just as quick. *I promise I'm okay. From what I hear, you guys have had a lot of calls tonight?*

Like you wouldn't believe. Then he sent her some emojis of a wolf howling at a full moon. He wasn't going to tell her about his injury because it wasn't even a technical stabbing, and he didn't want to worry her. He'd only needed a few Steri-Strips. She had enough to deal with. Even if she wasn't pregnant, he wouldn't tell her.

Good, stay safe.

You too. Then he tucked his phone away and headed out. He liked texting with Autumn, liked everything about her. He was still coming to terms with everything she'd told him about her life earlier in the evening. It stunned and touched him that she'd been so honest with him—and he knew that she was forbidden from telling him or anyone about her past.

He was surprised by her level of honesty, and he would never break her trust. The fact that she'd been open with him made him think that he had a chance with her. Because he wasn't giving up on them.

Not by a long shot.

CHAPTER TWENTY-ONE

"**Y**ou look like you could use a shot of espresso to go with your latte," Bianca said dryly as she took Autumn's order. Her long blonde hair was in its usual plaited braid down her back. The sleek, lean owner of Sweet Spot looked as if she'd gotten a full eight hours of sleep and a spa day.

Autumn wished she could relate. She lifted an eyebrow. "Thanks."

Bianca snorted softly. "Sorry, I'm not insulting you. You just look..."

"Tired? It's because I am." After the attempted break-in last night, she'd been too worried to sleep. She had someone coming out later today to fix her window, but it still didn't make her feel any better. She kept having random thoughts, worried that somehow Rand Coventry had faked his death, then made it all the way to Verona Bay and had tried to break into her house. Never mind how he would have found her. She simply hadn't been able to shut off her brain last night even though she'd known she was being ridiculous. The only bright spot had been the brief texts she and Lincoln had exchanged. She missed him this morning, wished she'd spent last night curled up in his arms.

"You want anything stronger than decaf?"

Yes, she thought, but shook her head. "I will take one of those double chocolate chip muffins."

"They're amazing, if I do say so myself. So what's going on? Are you worried about Lincoln? He'll be fine," she added. "He didn't even stay at the hospital or anything."

She blinked at the word hospital, a thread of alarm weaving through her. "What do you mean?"

Her friend stared at her as she set her to-go latte on the countertop. "Um... I just assumed you were worried about him."

"Why would I be worried?" She narrowed her gaze but Bianca turned away to pack up her muffin. "Bianca, come on." There were three people behind her in line but she didn't care if they overheard.

Bianca winced as she turned back around. "Look, I just heard through the grapevine this morning that he got stabbed last night. But it obviously must not have been too bad because he's at the station now." Then she quickly read off the total, looking a little guilt stricken.

Stabbed? Wordlessly Autumn set the cash on the countertop and grabbed her stuff, leaving her change as she hurried out.

Panic like she'd never known swelled up inside her, her heart racing as she hurried down the sidewalk. It took everything inside her not to full-on sprint down Main Street, which would've been pretty impossible in her sandals anyway. But... *stabbed?* They'd texted last night and he hadn't said a thing. It must have happened afterward or he would have told her.

My God, what was he doing at work if he'd been hurt like that? She couldn't control the wild beat of her heart and she didn't remember most of her half walk, half jog to the station.

Suddenly she was shoving the front door open into the lobby, the air-conditioning blasting her. She vaguely recognized the new admin assistant, Ellen. "I need to see Lincoln *now*," she snapped out, feeling crazy but unable to stop herself.

The woman gave her a startled look and pushed up slightly from her chair. "I just need to know who's asking for him," she stammered out.

"Sorry, my name's Autumn—"

Before she finished, Lincoln stepped out of his office, his eyebrows raised as he took her in. Her hair was probably wild around her face and she was out of breath. "Is everything okay?"

She raked her gaze over him, looking for any sign of injury. "You were stabbed last night?" she demanded much louder than she'd intended, her voice echoing around the room.

Lincoln winced and hurried to open up the little swinging half door that did nothing to separate the lobby from the back offices. "Come back to my office," he murmured, placing his hand at the small of her back as she stepped through. "Something smells good."

She simply stared at him in horror as they stepped inside his sparse office. "I don't want to talk about my muffin!" Trembles wracked her body, so she dropped her drink and pastry bag onto his desk.

"I'm okay, I promise." Gently, he guided her to one of his ugly brown chairs.

Her knees practically gave out as she sat, the chair making a crinkling sound under her. "So you're not denying that you were stabbed?" She looked him over again from head to toe in a completely clinical fashion.

"I wasn't stabbed. Whoever told you that was misinformed. We had a rough call out last night and I was barely nicked."

Unable to sit still, she shoved up, still not sure if she believed him. "Did you need stitches?"

"Steri-Strips."

"Those are the same thing."

"No they're not. I swear I'm fine." His voice was all calm and placating and for some reason, it got her even more worked up.

"Did this happen before or after we texted?"

He paused, his gorgeous green eyes narrowing slightly, as if he was debating his answer. "Before. I was actually at the hospital."

Dammit. "I know we're not together but I'm still going to have your baby!" Oh God, she knew she needed to get control of herself—she was never like this—but her emotions were wild. Someone had attacked him with a *knife* last night. And she was not handling it well. The thought of something happening to him?

She sucked in a breath, ordered herself to remain calm. She was worried simply because she cared for him, not because he was the father of her baby. She... cared for him way too much. "I'm sorry, I don't know what's wrong with me. I just... I wish you'd told me. I mean, you didn't even have to. I'm acting crazy, I know that."

He stepped forward, and in that moment, there was a predatory gleam in his eyes. Not one that scared her, one that made her feel... *Things.*

"I know how you feel about my job," he said quietly. "And like you said, you're pregnant. I didn't want to worry you needlessly. And I'm trying to say this in the most diplomatic way possible, but we're not together, so I'm not yours to worry about." There was no maliciousness in his words, just fact.

To her horror, tears stung her eyes, hot and blinding. Stupid, traitorous tears! She wasn't a crier, hadn't been her entire life, but pregnancy was wreaking havoc on her body. She didn't even feel like her body belonged to her anymore. She bawled the other day over a commercial featuring a mom and daughter cooking oatmeal cookies. It was so ridiculous. But Lincoln meant more to her than he would ever realize, and the thought of him being hurt tore her up inside almost as much as his words—a reminder that he wasn't hers and never would be.

"Hell. Don't cry." He cupped her cheeks gently, swiping away her tears.

"I'm not crying," she muttered.

"I can see that," he said, just a hint of amusement glittering in his gaze.

"These tears aren't for you."

"I'm sorry I didn't tell you," he said.

"You have nothing to be sorry for." She was the one overreacting, she knew that. It didn't make her emotions go away, however. They were still a riotous hurricane inside her. And with him so close, the scent of his Irish Spring soap teasing her, she wasn't thinking clearly. Not at all.

"I'm sorry anyway," he murmured, his gaze straying to her mouth.

Hers landed on his too, his delicious, wicked mouth she wanted more of.

Autumn didn't remember moving, just leaned forward at the same time he leaned down, crushing his mouth over hers in a harsh claiming.

There was no softness in him now as he took, his tongue teasing hers, his body pressing her back against his desk.

She automatically spread her thighs and hopped up on the edge, her dress pushing up as he slid in between her legs.

He tasted so familiar, like coffee and something sweet. Chocolate maybe. She moaned into his mouth as she clutched onto his shoulders, her nails digging in. She could have lost him last night. Even thinking that tore her up. She didn't want to let him go at all.

Suddenly he drew back, breathing hard as he watched her.

"We can't do this here," he rasped out. His chest rose and fell erratically as he looked down at her. "And since I'm pretty sure you haven't changed your mind about us, I don't think we can do this at all."

"I…" She wasn't sure where her head was at, felt far too emotional to make any decision. The fear of fully and completely falling for a man like Lincoln and then losing him to violence—last night being a good example—touched on the raw wound inside her. One that had never healed.

She was scared, she could admit it. Scared over a lot of things. But losing Lincoln? That was something she didn't know if she'd recover from. It was a constant struggle to hide her feelings from him. And if he knew how much power he had over her, he would easily break down the walls she'd erected between them.

"So what are you doing downtown today?" He expertly changed the subject as he stepped away from her and adjusted himself.

She tried not to notice his erection, tried to ignore the heat between her own legs that simply kissing him had brought on, and struggled to find her voice. "I'm teaching a class this morning. I stopped at the café and Bianca mentioned something about you getting stabbed." Then she'd run straight over here like a lunatic.

"Small-town gossip," he muttered.

Her eyes widened. "Oh my God, your employees definitely heard me yell that I was pregnant with your baby." And people had seen her run down here as if something was on fire. *Oh, no. No, no, no.*

To her surprise, he grinned. "They definitely did."

Her cheeks flushed hot and she realized that it would be all over town by the end of the day. Heck, by the end of her class this morning. She'd wanted to wait until she was through the first trimester to tell anyone. "I'm going to pretend that they didn't, and I'm just going to teach class today."

"Are you okay, honestly? You had a hell of a day yesterday what with... Everything you learned." She was glad he stayed vague. "And then with the break-in."

And that run-in with the jackass parent and the blown tire. She wasn't even sure if Lincoln knew about that and didn't want to bring it up now. "Yesterday was like an eternity. I swear Mercury is in retrograde or something. Did you guys find out anything about the break-in?" She had cameras on her front and back porches, but the would-be intruder had managed to avoid them, going for a window on the side of her house.

"No. I doubt they'll be back but if you want to stay with me—as friends only—you're more than welcome to. Both you and Shadow."

She shouldn't be surprised by his offer, but more tears materialized. Seriously, her body was betraying her. This was worse than morning sickness, she was certain.

"Please don't cry." He sounded almost panicked.

"Unfortunately I think all these crazy emotions are here to stay for the next few months."

He pulled her into a gentle hug, kissing the top of her head. "Come on, I'll walk you to the cultural center."

The way he held her so carefully made her wish things were different. He was exactly what she'd choose in her partner—if her life was normal. "You don't have to do that."

"I want to."

Feeling only a little embarrassed as she stepped out into the lobby with him, she noticed his assistant studiously avoided looking at either of them. Oh yeah, the woman had definitely heard Autumn's outburst.

Sighing at herself, she slipped her hand through Lincoln's arm. Friends did this, right?

Ugh. Who was she kidding? She wanted to be more than friends with Lincoln, and she always had. And soon the whole town would know their secret.

CHAPTER TWENTY-TWO

Tom Coventry hurried down the sidewalk in downtown Verona Bay, careful to keep his steps even.

He couldn't believe it. Ana Diaz—or Autumn, as she was calling herself these days—was actually *here* in the flesh. Looking at the pictures of her had been one thing, but actually seeing her in person, ten years after she'd taken everything, destroyed *everything*, was something else entirely.

It was clear she was chummy with law enforcement— he'd seen her walking with the sheriff hours ago—something he wasn't sure how he was going to handle. *Yet.* Because he'd already come this far. There was no turning back.

Now that he'd confirmed that she was in Verona Bay, he had to start putting his plan into action. He hadn't thought that far ahead, hadn't even been certain that she was alive. Tom hadn't allowed himself to hope that he'd finally be able to get his revenge.

All he knew was that he wanted her to suffer, to pay for what she'd done. She'd taken his whole career away. He'd wanted nothing more than to go into politics since he'd been twelve. His entire life, he'd been working toward his goals, taking one step at a time—leaping over some giant hurdles to get there. He'd married the right woman, provided everything for his son.

If only Rand had called him after that girl had died. He would have been able to dispose of her body. And he wouldn't have been caught. But his stupid, stupid son had decided to take matters into his own hands—while high on coke. Of course he'd screwed up.

Deep breaths, Tom ordered himself. If he allowed his mind to travel down that path, he would let his anger show. Right now, he had to be invisible. And for the most part he was. He wasn't a well-known senator. No, he worked at an exclusive financial firm and made millions a year, but he was still unknown to people in this pathetic, little town.

Even so, as he stepped into the local hardware shop, he automatically tugged his ball cap low. A place like this wouldn't have tons of security cameras, but he was going to do his due diligence.

Cruising the aisles, he started grabbing things he might need. Rope, tape, maybe a hammer. He already had a pistol and a knife, but simply shooting her would be too easy—way too easy for someone like her. She deserved all the pain and suffering he could mete out. Besides, a knife was quieter, and he wasn't interested in getting caught. No, he wanted his revenge, then to go back to his life.

"That's what I heard," he overheard a petite blonde-haired woman telling a taller man as they picked out doorknobs down the aisle from him.

He sidestepped around them, not caring what they were talking about. The people here were nobodies.

"I've always thought they should get together," the woman said. "It's about time our sheriff found someone to settle down with. I just know his mom is going to be thrilled."

At the mention of the word sheriff, Tom paused and pretended to look at light bulbs.

"You don't even know if it's true, Betsy," the man muttered, picking out a deadbolt and tossing it into the cart.

"I know what I heard. And it sounds like Autumn is pregnant too, so I predict wedding bells soon."

"Even if she is pregnant, it doesn't mean they're getting married or anything."

"Speaking of marriage," the woman continued, making the man choke on air.

Tom had heard enough, however. Could that one busybody be right? When he'd seen the sheriff walking down the street with her that morning, she'd had her hand on his arm.

Well, wasn't this news interesting. It didn't change anything for him. If anything, her being pregnant was even better.

She'd taken his family from him. Now he would take hers.

CHAPTER TWENTY-THREE

Autumn knocked on Lincoln's door, glad he'd asked her over tonight. She'd texted him earlier when she'd seen him arrive home at five to ask if he'd wanted company. They were having a kid together and she knew that she needed to reach out more—and she was embarrassed about the way she'd acted earlier that morning. She didn't think he was upset with her, but she still wanted to make sure things were good with them. She didn't care what anyone else in town thought or if the gossip mill had started, she just cared what Lincoln thought.

So she'd ordered takeout from his favorite Italian place.

He opened the door a few moments later, smelling like Irish Spring soap and something that was all him. Even though she'd just seen him only hours ago, her heart rate kicked up nonetheless as she drank him in. In dark jeans, a gray T-shirt and bare feet, he looked... hell, sexy. He always did, no matter what.

"Come on in," he said, eyeing the big brown bag she held. "Please tell me you brought enough to share."

She let out a startled laugh as he shut the door behind her. "No, I'm just going to eat all this deliciousness in front of you without sharing."

He plucked the bag out of her hand and headed to the kitchen. "You must have read my mind because I was going to order takeout from Taste of Rome too."

"I'm glad you're hungry because I'm starving. I forgot to eat for lunch and my stomach is definitely starting to feel it."

"No sickness yet?" he asked as he started pulling down plates.

"No, thankfully," she said. "Hopefully it won't happen." It was weird, she constantly felt as if she was on the edge of getting sick, an underlying nausea that went away once she ate, for the most part.

"My mom didn't have it with me. Something she likes to remind my brothers of." He pulled out silverware and glasses, set them on the center island.

A pang of yearning slid through her. The thought of spending all her evenings like this, with him? Yeah, she liked the sound of that. "So... I got a call from my handler. There was something wrong with the DNA test. Looks like it got corrupted."

He paused to look at her. "Corrupted?"

"Yeah. Well, the DNA for both of the prisoners was correct—ish, I guess. Some of the samples gave a weird reading or... something. I don't really understand the science of it. But Coventry's DNA was found at the crash so it looks like a botched escape attempt." That made her feel a whole lot better. Especially since Erica seemed to think that Rand was collateral damage. She didn't want to talk about it, but she had wanted to share the news with Lincoln. "My handler said she'd let me know once they get the new results back. So, can I help with anything?"

"Nope, just sit. I've got this."

Since her feet hurt, she wasn't going to push. She took a seat at the center island. His kitchen was pristine, clearly having been renovated in the last few years, and was very aesthetically pleasing. Dark gray shaker cabinets, light gray and white granite center island with a waterfall effect, heavy exposed beams on the ceiling and three glass pendant lights hanging above the island. Everything about the room was soothing to the artist side of her.

"What would it take for you to give us a real chance?"

His blunt question took her off guard. She shifted in her seat as she tried to formulate a response.

He continued, watching her closely. "Do you want me to quit my job?"

"What? No! I would never ask you to give up your career. I lost part of mine, so I know how hard that is."

He continued getting them drinks so she pulled out the food from the bag, desperate to have something to do with her hands. She set the containers on trivets in the middle of the island top so they could serve themselves.

"You lost your career?" he asked quietly.

She liked that she could be honest with him now. "For the most part, yes. They didn't even want me doing anything art adjacent in my life, but I made it clear that wasn't happening. It would have been like giving up a part of my soul, and honestly, it wouldn't have been worth it to go into the program. It would have slowly killed me anyway. But yes, I was huge into photography. I'd started building my portfolio, had a well-known mentor working with me to get my first real show off the ground. I still love photography, but I don't sell my work or have a website or anything like that." She didn't have *any* social media.

He set a glass of ice water in front of her. "I've got sweet tea or hot tea if you want?"

"This is perfect." He seemed to know her well. Even before the pregnancy, she'd pretty much only drank water throughout the day. As a teacher, she liked to stay hydrated.

"Tell me more about your life before," he said quietly, though it came out as a question.

"Before... everything, I had just graduated college with full honors. My whole neighborhood was proud of me. My mom... She would've been proud too, if she'd been alive." She cleared her throat and speared the spaghetti noodles that came with her eggplant parmesan, twisting them onto her fork. "I was working for this man named Hector. He was my mentor, but also like a father figure to me. Leaving him was one of the hardest things I had to do as well. It was like leaving family even if we aren't blood. He's a fairly well-known artist, at least in the art world. You probably wouldn't know his name but you might recognize some of his pictures."

His specialty was capturing real-life moments and they were always so full of color. One of her favorites of his was one he'd taken at a local festival. A bunch of young kids had been releasing brightly colored balloons into the air, and he'd captured the absolute joy on their faces. It had been reprinted, and she knew he made nice passive royalties on them—she had one herself.

"I'd like to see them. I'd like to see your work too. Any of it that you feel comfortable showing me, of course."

She could hear the sincerity in Lincoln's voice and something inside her shifted again, knowing that he actually cared about who she was. And being able to tell him about all parts of her life was so freeing. Another pang punched through her. She wished… for too much.

She cleared her throat. "Anyway, when I entered the program, they had very strict rules about how I couldn't get a job that links me to my old life, how I *definitely* couldn't continue my photography career. I have to keep a very low profile online, absolutely no social media, just common sense stuff. But teaching art was a compromise of sorts." She shook her head slightly as she remembered the arguments she'd gotten into with Erica about it. "They definitely weren't happy about it but they had to live with it. I knew the risk and accepted it. It was either that or I didn't enter the program." It was the only thing she hadn't been willing to compromise on.

He nodded, listening intently, but she wanted to know more about *him*.

"I want to know more about you, but first, how's your *stab* wound?"

His mouth kicked up. "It's not a stab wound, and I'm fine. It itches a little, that's it."

"Okay," she murmured. "So how did you get into law enforcement?"

"You know all about Serenity, obviously," he started. She nodded because everyone in town knew what had happened with her. "Yeah. She's so tough and brave." Like this fierce tornado.

"From what it sounds like, so are you."

Autumn's mouth curved up into a smile as she cut off a piece of the eggplant Parmesan. "I wasn't digging for compliments, promise."

"I know. Anyway, we were pretty tight in college, and then her sister died—was murdered—and everything I thought I knew about the world changed in an instant. I knew I wanted to help people. So I got my degree, joined the Marines as an officer, then when I got out, I moved back home. From there I was still trying to decide if I wanted to go into construction with Lucas or move somewhere else to start in law enforcement. My mother had the bright idea that I should run for sheriff. I thought she was crazy, but I was the youngest sheriff elected." A smile played at his lips, as if he was trying not to brag.

"I heard what a jackass the sheriff before you was. I've seen the way you've built a relationship with the community and it's impressive. It's not like that everywhere," she added. "Not where I lived in California, and not in the few places I've lived since then."

"I make a choice every day to be able to look myself in the mirror at night. And I care about this town and the people in it. My family has lived here for four generations."

"You have a good family. You're lucky," she added, unable to keep the wistfulness out of her voice. She'd met his brothers and mom and they were all wonderful.

"They'll be your family too, soon."

She paused, digesting his words even as she dismissed them. She knew that he'd just been making an offhand comment about her being family now too, but they weren't. They would be family to the child they had together, but she was just a woman he'd gotten pregnant. A friend.

"Speaking of... How would you feel about having dinner at my parents' ranch tomorrow night? I'm going to be there for our Sunday dinner, and it might make it easier to get things over with and meet them all officially now. My mom heard something about you being pregnant and... I couldn't lie to her."

Oh, wow. She'd gotten calls from a few friends—including Adeline and Serenity—and confirmed her pregnancy. She just hadn't thought about his parents finding out for some reason. So, that was definitely out there. "Will Serenity be there?"

"Of course."

"I'll go. I mean, I would've gone anyway, but it will be nice to have a friendly face there."

"Hey, I'm a friendly face too." His mouth curved up as he took a bite of his pasta.

She laughed lightly and dug into her food. Things with him were so easy, and it was soooo easy for her to imagine what it would be like to have a real relationship—one that was more than friendship. But what happened if things went haywire? What if he went out on a call and didn't come back? She knew she was getting all up in her head but it was impossible not to worry. Because he had a huge extended family and he was the sheriff of the town. What if something happened between them and they split up... There were so many ways that things could go wrong.

"You look like you're lost in thought," he said before taking a sip of his own water.

"I'm sorry. Letting my mind wander." She was actively looking for reasons to keep the wall between them in place.

He watched her cautiously, but didn't push. Instead, he said, "I have something important to ask you."

Her stomach muscles tightened. "Okay."

"What's your favorite ice cream?"

She blinked before letting out another laugh—something she seemed to do a lot around him. Laugh. Be free. Damn him, he was so far under her skin it wasn't funny. "Mississippi Mud for sure. It's got everything a girl needs."

"I'll make sure to get some stocked."

Oh hell, the man was perfect.

CHAPTER TWENTY-FOUR

"You look beautiful," Lincoln said as they strode up to the front door of his parents' house.

"I still think I should have worn a sweater or something." Autumn had opted for a casual yellow and blue summer dress but all of her tattoos were on display and now she was questioning her choice of outfit.

He shot her a confused look. "Why?" Then his gaze swept over her and the hunger lingering there was so evident she felt it like a caress. She wondered if he was even aware of the way he looked at her, always with a hint of desire.

"Because of my tattoos."

He blinked in surprise. "It's not 1952 and my parents don't care."

She snickered softly. "Well a lot of people do care." Not anyone who mattered, but still. "You wouldn't believe some of the comments I've gotten while out just minding my own business, like grocery shopping."

"Here in Verona Bay?"

"No, though I have gotten a few scandalized looks from some nice church ladies," she said, rolling her eyes. She liked that Lincoln not only didn't care about her tattoos, but seemed to like them. When they'd spent that night together, he'd kissed every one of them, taking his time.

He started to respond, when the front door opened and Louise Jordan tugged both of them inside. She gave her son a tight hug and, as she stepped back, said, "I can't believe you knocked on the door. You have a key."

He shrugged, looking uncomfortable. "I just wanted to announce that we were here."

She patted his cheek gently. "Is it because last time you walked in on me and your dad—"

"Mom!"

For the first time since she'd met him, Lincoln's cheeks flushed red.

Autumn let out a startled burst of laughter. "Oh my God, you walked in on your parents?" She blurted it out before she could stop herself.

His mother shook her head. "We were fully clothed. But Lincoln can be such a prude sometimes."

She couldn't help it, she giggled, because the Lincoln she knew was definitely *not* a prude. Nope, he was creative with a slightly dirty mouth.

"Can we please stop having this conversation and move into the kitchen or somewhere other than out here on the doorstep?" he grumbled, looking adorable.

This was a side to him Autumn had never seen, and she liked it.

Louise took Autumn's hand and pulled her into the house. "I'm so happy you're here tonight. It's very rare that I get all my kids in one place. Everyone is so busy, us included."

"I'm glad to be here too." From the outside the place looked huge, and inside... it was more gorgeous. Shiny dark oak floors, high ceilings, and horse- and ranch-themed art—she recognized a couple of the artists. "And thank you for inviting me." She handed Louise a bottle of wine that Lincoln said his mom would definitely like.

"You didn't have to do this, but thank you."

As they entered the kitchen, Serenity slid off a barstool and immediately pulled her into a tight hug. "I'm so glad you're here. Lucas just told me that Linc was bringing you. He's actually about to take Harper out for a ride on one of the horses before dinner. Did you want to go?"

She couldn't stop her horrified expression, which made Louise and Lincoln both laugh.

"You don't like horses?" Lincoln's voice held a thread of surprise.

"I think they're beautiful, majestic animals. But I have no desire to ride one. I've tried twice and both times it was awkward and uncomfortable. I'm pretty sure they could sense my fear too." She was perfectly happy watching others ride them. Or even painting or photographing them, but she was giving them a wide berth.

Louise nodded as Lincoln started pouring drinks for all of them. "They can definitely sense your emotions," he said.

"Sweetheart, why don't you head to the barn with the rest of the boys and Harper?" Louise said without looking over her shoulder at Lincoln. It sounded kind of like a question, but was very clearly an order.

He paused, and looked at the three of them. "Is that a polite way of kicking me out of the house?"

"Yes, and if you push it, I won't be so polite."

Autumn watched their interaction with amusement and a bit of longing. She'd loved her mom but had never been super close to her. Her mom had had a hole inside her that nothing could ever fill. She'd looked for peace in the arms of abusive men. The definition of insanity was doing the same thing over and over and expecting a different outcome, something her mom had perfected to an art. And it had broken Autumn's heart. She was determined not to fall into the same traps as her mom had, to be a better role model.

From what she knew of Louise, and from what she could see in the three boys that the woman had helped raise with her husband, the woman was incredible. And part of Autumn was sad that she would never truly be part of their family. She would be more like an adjacent member.

Not necessarily, that little voice in her head whispered. She shut it down, however.

To her surprise, Lincoln kissed the top of Autumn's head. "I've got my phone on me if my mother drives you crazy," he murmured before leaving.

Feeling way off kilter, she simply sat at the countertop with Serenity and wrapped her fingers around the glass Lincoln had set in front of her. His mom hadn't said anything about the pregnancy so maybe she wouldn't at all. Maybe it would be this thing that they just avoided completely tonight.

"You are so good for my boy," Louise said as soon as the back door shut.

"Oh, we're not... That is, we are *friends*." Friends who were having a baby together.

Louise simply smiled at her and nodded. "Oh, I know. He told me the same thing. But I still think you guys are adorable together."

She cleared her throat and took a sip of her drink, shooting a glance at Serenity, who was smiling into her own glass of wine. Autumn missed wine.

And coffee.

And sex with Lincoln.

"Is there anything I can do to help with dinner? Make the salad?" Whatever was in the oven smelled delicious.

"You sit right there with Serenity. I just have to put the salad together and it won't take long. By the time I'm done they'll probably all be back and acting like starving wolves, so enjoy this quiet."

"It's true. They act more like hyenas when food is around, and my daughter is the worst of them," Serenity said on a laugh.

She watched as Louise pulled out lettuce, tomatoes, cucumbers, and a bunch of other fixings. It felt weird not to be helping out but the truth was, she was exhausted more often than not now. She used to run on caffeine and energy, but the little peanut was taking it out of her.

"I know it's not my business, and if you want, just tell me to shut up," Louise started. "But have you guys decided if you're going to find out the sex of the baby?"

She blinked. Okay, so they weren't going to gloss over it. She was surprised Louise was being so open about it. Surprised and grateful, because at least it gave her an opening to talk about her pregnancy. "Actually I hadn't really thought about it. But I would like to know just because I'm curious. Lincoln hasn't mentioned anything though, so I don't know how he feels." She just knew that he wanted to come to all of her doctor's appointments.

"I liked knowing because it was easier to pick a name," Serenity said before taking a sip of her drink. Then she glanced at her cell phone, which buzzed across the countertop. "If you guys will excuse me, I'm going to head out to the barn. Harper apparently needs me."

Panic punched through Autumn at the thought of being alone with Lincoln's mom. Sure, the woman seemed perfectly nice, but they'd never spent any alone time together. Louise had taken a few of her classes and she knew her just from around town but that was it. Now she was pregnant with her youngest son's baby—what if she really hated Autumn?

"You should see your face," Louise said as the door shut behind Serenity.

"What?"

"Honey, I'm not going to bite. And I promise I will try to stay out of your business and not give you any parenting advice that you *don't* ask for. I had a nightmare of a mother-in-law and I never want to be like that—I mean, I know you and Lincoln aren't together," she added. "But you're going to be in our lives. And we are very excited to get to know you. No pressure or anything, but if you need help with anything baby related, just let me know. I won't push, but the offer is there so feel free to reach out."

Somehow that was the perfect thing to say and once again, to her utter horror, tears sprang to her eyes. "Dammit," she muttered.

Louise quickly grabbed a paper towel and handed her one across the countertop. "I remember those days. With Easton I was like a leaky faucet that just wouldn't shut off. Lincoln was actually a dream when I was pregnant with him. Lucas, on the other hand, talk about morning sickness. Have you had any?"

She shook her head. "I'm just tired a lot. And it's weird not being able to drink coffee."

"Having a kid will change everything for you. Especially if that kid grows up to be an adrenaline junkie. Or goes into a dangerous profession." She shook her head slightly.

"How do you deal with it?" In that moment, Autumn realized that all three of Louise's boys had gone into fairly dangerous professions and all had served in different branches of the military. Easton was a firefighter, Lincoln was sheriff and Lucas was in construction, which in itself had a lot of dangers.

"Keeping busy, staying active in the community, drinking wine," she said on a laugh. "I'm not gonna lie, there were some nights I cried alone in the shower because I didn't want my husband to know how hard it was dealing with all of them being gone and in danger. In some cases, I wasn't even able to have contact with them at different times. But kids have to live their own lives," she said on a shrug.

"Very true." She hadn't even thought about motherhood, it had always been more abstract than anything. Now she was trying to get through this pregnancy, but after... oh God, she would have a tiny life to take care of. For so long she'd just been afraid, looking over her shoulder. Then she'd finally settled in Verona Bay and was starting to allow herself to feel as if she could have a real life. Now, to be responsible for someone else, yeah, it was a little scary.

"I know I said that I wouldn't give you any advice, but I might give you *one* little piece if you're open to it?" Louise didn't look up from dicing her tomato.

"Okay."

"Some of my friends have deprived themselves of real relationships, real joy because of their own fear. So if you let fear take over your life, and keep up walls, and don't take a chance on... well, relationships, there's a good chance you might regret it for the rest of your life."

It was clear that was all she was going to say, and Autumn appreciated it. She sipped her drink, feeling a little awkward. Her feelings for Lincoln didn't matter.

"You know what, I actually might need some help," Louise said into the lull. "Would you mind grabbing the banana peppers from the fridge? Easton can't get enough of those."

"Of course." She slid off the stool, glad to have something to do with her hands. As they worked together, she realized that was... Christmas music playing in the background. "You're playing Christmas music in September?"

"Oh honey, I play it year round. Drives my husband crazy."

It was kind of nice, Autumn thought. Soothing even. This was the kind of household she wished she'd grown up in. Maybe if she had, she wouldn't be so damn afraid.

* * *

"So has my family completely terrified you of ever going over there again?" Lincoln's question sounded only half-joking as they headed home in his truck later.

"Tonight was fun. I liked watching your family dynamics. It's pretty clear that Harper has your parents wrapped around her finger. Not that I blame them, she's adorable." Serenity had really nailed the parent thing with that kid. She was adorable, sweet, and kind.

"Serenity seriously impresses me."

"Is it weird for your brother that you and her are such good friends?" She'd seen them together well before tonight, and it was clear they had a sweet sibling type relationship.

Laughing lightly, he shook his head. "No, but you're very astute. I think there's only been one or two times where Lucas was weirdly jealous. But I think that's just a Jordan man thing."

"What do you mean?"

"Being protective and possessive of our women." He shot her a sideways glance.

Oh. The heat in his eyes was blatant now. Not simmering anymore. "You don't seem very..." She tried to think of the right way to phrase it. It was weird because he had alpha qualities, but for the most part he seemed very low-key. Well, until he wasn't.

He seemed to understand what she was saying. "If I went all alpha and possessive on you, you would kick me to the curb."

She lifted a shoulder because it was true. If he'd acted all he-man crazy, she never would have given him a chance. As it was, he was always so patient and kind. And sexy, she could never forget that part.

As he pulled into her driveway, she cleared her throat nervously. Tonight had shifted things for her. She'd seen what they could have together, what they could be together. Yes, she was still terrified of the future, of losing Lincoln. But she could lose him no matter what. And what happened if, later on down the line, he ended up with someone else? It would tear her apart to watch him be with another woman. She just needed to go for it.

"Look, I would like to go out on a date with you." After tonight she knew that she needed to get over herself and give them a chance. Because she would absolutely regret it if she didn't.

The truck jerked forward as he slammed on the brakes. "What?"

"I... Would like to give us a chance. I'm open to trying dating." It terrified her because if things got all pear-shaped, then life would suck for a while, but his mom had been right. Autumn didn't want to deprive herself of a real future because of fear. She was always honest and bold in her art. She should be in her life too. Hell, she'd testified in court against a monster, given up her entire life and identity to put that bastard behind bars. She didn't want to give up a shot at happiness because she was afraid of "what if" might happen to him. Or to them. She could what if herself to death.

"How about tomorrow? I'll take you out anywhere you want to go, or cook for you." He didn't miss a beat, jumped right into making plans, something that made her smile.

"I'm teaching a class tomorrow downtown, but what about Tuesday? I like the idea of you cooking."

"Deal. I've got the night off, and I would love to cook for you. With no expectations afterward," he tacked on. "I mean, if you decide you want to get naked with me again, I'm totally in."

She grinned at the mischievous glint in his eyes. The thought of getting naked with him again was absolutely fantastic. The last two days she'd been ridiculously horny and while she wanted to blame it on her pregnancy, she knew it was just because she'd been around Lincoln, and he got her all hot and bothered.

Her gaze fell to his mouth and a slow-burning wild-fire started at her toes, working its way up until her breasts felt heavy, tight. She'd had fantasies about his mouth. "Would it be inappropriate for a good night kiss before our official first date?" she whispered. She didn't want to wait until tomorrow.

"Hell no." His voice was husky, his eyes dilated as he watched her.

She leaned forward at the same time he did, their lips touching, electricity arching between them.

And just like that, he took over, tugging her over into his seat so that she was straddling him. She liked that he took charge at the right time.

As she rubbed over his growing erection, dampness rushed between her legs. Her scrap of material thong and his pants were no real barrier between them, and he was so damn hard. Knowing that she affected him as much as he did her, made her light-headed.

She might even be able to get off if she rubbed against him like a cat in heat.

"I want you so bad," he growled against her mouth, his fingers clenching around her hips with a possessive need.

At those words, her nipples beaded even harder, her arousal spiking. She clutched onto his shoulders. "I want you too." Those words weren't enough to convey just how badly she wanted him to slide inside her, to feel him thrusting hard and deep, to completely fill her.

She started rolling her hips against his as he reached between their bodies and cupped her covered mound.

"You feel so good," she rasped out against his mouth. But she needed more.

He shoved her panties to the side to cup her mound and groaned again when he slid a finger through her slick folds. "Damn, you're so wet."

And it was all because of him. She couldn't talk at that moment, not when he slid a finger inside her. She started riding his finger as he began strumming her clit with his thumb. He rubbed her in tight little circles, clearly re-membering what she liked. She clenched around him, still needing more. As she bit his bottom lip, he added another finger.

Now he nipped at *her* bottom lip, teasing, tasting, as he slowly curled his fingers inside her. Combined with the way he was rubbing her clit, it wouldn't take her long now. And the fact that they were in her driveway made her feel like a teenager.

Not that she'd ever done this as a teenager. This was fun and freeing and she loved that she was doing this with Lincoln. With him, she felt free and safe.

She wanted to tell him how much he meant to her, how scared she was to take this chance with him, but that he was worth it. No words would come, however, as her climax started to build.

He slid another finger inside her and she lost it, falling into that well of pleasure as a kaleidoscope of colors exploded behind her eyes. Her orgasm hit hard and sharp, probably because she'd been fantasizing about this for nine weeks. Still, she was surprised at the intensity of her orgasm as her toes curled under the force.

"Oh my God," she whispered when it faded. "Pregnant orgasms are a good thing."

He chuckled slightly, though it came out kind of pained as he shifted his hips up once, trying to adjust himself.

Knowing he had to be in discomfort—and wanting to make sure he got just as much pleasure as she had—she quickly freed his thick length and started stroking him off with her hands. She wanted to go down on him, but there was no room.

He crushed his mouth to hers as she wrapped her fingers around him. She loved how thick and heavy he was. He pulsed under her grip as she stroked him, over and over. The tight space made things more intimate and the way he growled against her mouth told her that he wouldn't be long.

The harder she stroked, the more unleashed he became, his kisses wild and hungry as he finally came all over her fingers and his shirt.

Breathing hard, he looked up at her through heavy-lidded eyes, a sated smile on his face. "That was hot," he murmured.

It definitely was. And she loved seeing him like this, completely satisfied and relaxed. It gave her hope for their future. "That seems like a nice precursor to our date."

"I'm going to taste you next time." His statement was full of promise and heat.

Fire sparked through her at his words. Though she was terrified to take a chance with him, she was going to do it. Even if deep down she was worried that as soon as she allowed herself to be happy, the universe would rip everything away from her once again.

Lincoln was most definitely worth the risk.

CHAPTER TWENTY-FIVE

Adeline nearly jerked in surprise when she saw Mac pulling into the parking lot of the auto body shop place. Sliding her sunglasses on, she got out of her car and braced herself to see him. Every time she saw him, she thought maybe her reaction to him would lessen, but nope. He was still huge and sexy.

As she reached the sidewalk in front of the shop, he'd already gotten out of his Bronco.

"Adeline, hey," he said, bounding up onto the sidewalk looking as delicious as ever.

His sleeves were shoved up to his elbows, showing off those damn forearms. Seriously, the forearm game was going to kill her.

"Hey... How's Joe?" She'd heard through the grapevine that he'd been released and was doing well. But she'd felt weird checking in since she was basically just his tutor.

"Good. Fully recovered and staying at his girlfriend's tonight." Mac shook his head slightly. "Apparently they made up after their argument."

The girl had been there during the search effort, and it was clear that she'd been worried. "That's great," Adeline said. Then she stood there feeling awkward as she stared up at him. At that moment, she was very grateful for her sunglasses.

"I wanted to call you," he blurted.

"Oh... why? I mean..." Well, *why* would he have called her?

He rubbed a hand over the back of his neck. "To say thank you again. And to ask you out on a date," he rushed out.

She blinked, staring at him in surprise. First, because he was asking her out, and second, because he seemed nervous. Sex-on-a-stick Mac Collins was nervous? About asking her out? "On a date?" She winced at herself because she was basically just repeating him now.

"Yeah. I've wanted to ask you out for a while."

She snorted softly. No way. "Pretty sure you didn't even know I was alive." The words were out before she could stop herself.

"Oh, I've noticed you." His voice dropped an octave, his gaze sliding over her like an intimate caress.

Oh... oh, hell. A frisson of heat slid through her, but just as quickly, fear popped up in its place. Not fear of him, just her past. Being able to fantasize about Mac without any consequences had been therapeutic. He hadn't known she was alive, or at least that was what she'd *thought*. So it had been easy to indulge in a harmless crush and fantasies. Soooo very easy. But... he actually wanted to go out with her? Oh, no. Reality was so much different.

She took a slight step backward. "I don't know," she said quickly.

"No pressure or anything. I just thought maybe... There was a spark between us?"

Okay, so he'd felt that too. She cleared her throat, trying to figure out what to say, when the door opened and, bless her, Autumn walked out.

Her friend looked surprised when she spotted her. "Hey girl. Are you having car issues?" she asked, then seemed to notice Mac for the first time. "Oh, hey Mac."

How anyone could miss him, Adeline couldn't imagine. Her gaze always seemed to be drawn to him like that proverbial moth to a flame.

"Hey, Autumn," he murmured, barely glancing at her friend.

"I heard Joe has recovered fully and is doing great," she continued.

He gave a polite smile and nodded. "He is, thank you." Then he gave Adeline an unreadable look before nodding politely and murmuring that he needed to head inside.

"Did I interrupt something?" Autumn asked quietly, low enough that Adeline barely heard her.

"Ah, nope. Nothing." Only the best thing that had happened to her in forever. Even though she'd been afraid to take it.

"Sure didn't look like nothing. If you get to harass me about Lincoln, I totally get to harass you about Mac."

"What are you doing here anyway?" She hoped changing the subject would work.

To her surprise, Autumn's expression darkened. "I blew out my tire a couple days ago. So I brought it in to order a new one. The mechanic thinks... that maybe someone shot it out. I was on Industrial Road, you know, that backcountry one?"

Frowning, Adeline nodded. "I do know. I know jackasses like to illegally hunt back there. Or take potshots at the speed limit signs." She worked with the local shelter and was friends with one of the vets, and they'd dealt with hunting dogs getting shot by accident by morons who had no business handling guns. Or dogs. Or basically being in civilized society at all.

"Yeah, me too. Still... Kind of scary."

"Have you told Lincoln about it?"

"Not yet, but I'm going to."

She nodded slightly as she stepped back down on the pavement, falling in step with Autumn into the parking lot.

"What are you doing? Autumn asked.

"Nothing. I changed my mind about getting my oil changed today."

Autumn simply lifted an eyebrow. "Did you change your mind because of that sexy Mac Collins?"

"Better not let Lincoln hear you calling another man sexy." She actually didn't like anyone calling *Mac* sexy—though he was.

"You better mind your business," she shot back.

Adeline laughed and shook her head. "Glad to see your pregnancy isn't slowing down that smart mouth."

"Are you coming to the class tonight?"

"No, but I gave my extra ticket to Serenity. She said she'd bring someone with her. I picked up an extra tutoring shift and though I hate to miss your class, it won't hold."

"All right, I'll see you later in the week then."

Adeline nodded and got into her car. As she did, she felt ridiculous for leaving, but if she stepped inside that auto body shop, she would have to make small talk with Mac Collins, and she did *not* have that in her.

She couldn't believe he'd actually asked her out, couldn't believe he thought she was attractive enough to ask out. Or that she'd turned him down. He was like this walking, talking sex god. She'd once seen him without his shirt—by accident—and that memory was burned into her psyche.

But her taste in men ran toward the epic side of awful. So she was going to save herself some heartache and say no. Though he'd probably just let it drop. Or she hoped he would. She just hoped it wasn't awkward the next time she went over there to tutor Joe.

As she pulled out of the parking lot, she shelved that thought. She had more important things to deal with than a silly crush that wasn't going to go anywhere.

Because she wouldn't let it.

CHAPTER TWENTY-SIX

Lincoln watched Autumn from his seat behind the canvas, barely able to concentrate on anything but her the whole night. She was a great instructor who paid attention to everyone in the class. She'd come over a few times to help him out tonight and every time she did, her cheeks flushed an adorable shade of pink, and all he could think about was how her cheeks had flushed pink when he'd made her come last night in the front seat of his truck.

He'd definitely surprised her by showing up tonight, but when Serenity had told him she had an extra ticket, he'd jumped at the chance.

He'd gone for very simple and had chosen a butterfly to paint, figuring it would look good in the nursery. Though whenever he thought of setting up a nursery, he didn't want their baby to have two, one at her house and one at his. People co-parented all the time and it was fine, and deep down he knew it was too soon to ask her to move in—the thought of that was *insane*. They hadn't even gone on a real date yet. They were going on one tomorrow, but he knew that the future was still up in the air and he didn't want to get ahead of himself.

Still, he liked the thought of living with her. The thought of waking up to her every morning got his heart racing.

Especially after last night.

He added a little note at the bottom corner as he finished his colorful painting and when Autumn moved in behind him, he looked up at her to see what she thought. He had almost no skills when it came to painting, but he could follow instructions, and she'd sketched out four different options for people to choose from tonight.

Her eyes widened at his little note that said "from your daddy" at the bottom.

"That's really sweet," she whispered, squeezing his shoulder gently.

He pinned her in place with his stare. He wished they were alone right now, that everyone in this class would just leave so he could take her right on her desk, bury his head between her legs until she was crying out his name in pleasure.

"Oh my gosh, that is the sweetest thing ever," Serenity said as she came to stand next to Autumn.

He rubbed the back of his neck as a couple more women came over and looked at the painting, oohing over it. This was just for Autumn.

She leaned down, her sweet scent teasing him as she whispered, "That's what happens when you're so adorable." Then she straightened and started walking toward the front of the room. His gaze followed, unable to *not* look at her. "Alright everybody, that's it for the night. You guys know the drill, just leave your canvases here and you can come pick them up anytime tomorrow after ten."

After that, the class started closing down very quickly, with people washing their brushes and tidying up their stations with an efficiency that told him most, if not all of the people here, had done this before.

He took his time, dragging his feet cleaning until everyone was gone. He didn't want to wait until tomorrow night for his date with her and he wasn't letting her walk to her car alone. Especially since she'd mentioned about her tire potentially being shot out. The fact that Coventry was dead made him feel better, but he still didn't like that the mechanic had thought her tire blowout might not be an accident. He knew how jackasses hunted illegally on Industry Road, but the whole thing didn't sit right with him.

"So how'd you like the class?" Autumn said as she came to stand at the sink with him. Tonight she'd worn a loose-fitting, paint-splattered red dress with thin straps and yellow llamas all over it. It was clearly one of her work dresses but every time she moved, it shifted, pulling taut over her full breasts. Her pregnancy wasn't showing yet, not in an obvious way, but her breasts already seemed fuller.

"It was fun."

"Really?" Her tone was dubious.

He grinned. "Yeah. I liked getting to see you in action. You're a good teacher." Not that he'd ever doubted it. Everyone always had good things to say about her teaching and she'd pulled in a lot of people to the cultural center from her classes alone. People talked in small towns and she was very well liked here. "And I plan to hang out until you're done and walk you to your car."

She gave him a soft smile. "Thank you. The parking lot is well lit, but I do appreciate it."

Taking a chance, he bent down and brushed his mouth over hers, giving her plenty of time to pull back. He had no idea what they were at this point, but he knew he didn't want to go another second without kissing her. They were in a weird sort of limbo between friends and lovers. She was having his baby but they weren't exactly together, she'd just agreed to a date. But they'd also brought each other to orgasm last night in the front of his truck and would be raising a child together.

It was enough for anyone to get whiplash.

After everything she'd told him about her past, he understood her hesitance, but it didn't mean he had to like it.

Thankfully she leaned into him, clutching onto his shirt as she met his lips with her soft full ones. He nipped her bottom lip as he slid his hands down to her hips and pulled her flush against him. She had to feel his reaction to her—it was impossible to hide.

"What are you doing to me?" she groaned as she slightly pulled back, her breathing erratic.

"I'll do anything to you that you want," he murmured.

"I just mean, you, me, *us*. Are we crazy to try anything?"

"I think we might have done things out of order, but I don't think we're crazy. And who cares if we are? I want you, you want me, and we're having a baby together. I want to give this thing between us a shot. The real question is, are you willing to?"

She watched him for a long moment. "I am. And I already locked the front door," she whispered.

He blinked down at her, surprised at the raw heat that flared in her brown eyes. He'd just meant to kiss her briefly, to get a taste of her to tide him over until tomorrow because he was an addict where she was concerned.

"Yeah?" he growled low in his throat.

"Oh yeah. And all the windows in my office have blackout curtains. We have privacy."

He scooped her up into his arms, not about to turn away from this chance. "No one else will show up tonight?"

She shook her head.

Heart pounding, he hurried out into the hallway and straight across to her office. He kicked the door shut with his foot, his eyes on her face the whole time. She was finally letting him in. There was a shift between them—he could feel it. And he was grabbing this chance with both hands.

She quickly wiggled out of his arms and moved a stack of canvases while he picked up a couple boxes full of sample paints off her desk and slid them to the floor.

Then he lifted her up onto the desk as he leaned over her body, pinning her in place as he devoured her mouth with his own. She tasted sweet, like the chocolate he'd seen her snacking on earlier. Since he didn't want to rush things, he kept his hands planted firmly on her desk as he leaned over her, teasing his tongue against hers.

She wrapped her arms and legs around him, rolling her hips against his erection.

Screw going slow. "Gotta taste you again," he managed to rasp out against her mouth. His whole body burned with the need to take her right here.

She rolled her hips against his in response. He couldn't tear his mouth from hers yet, so he slid his hands under her dress and grasped the edges of her thong. It didn't take long to tug them down her legs and toss them aside.

Though he couldn't stop the energy humming through him, he slowly and gently lifted her left leg and kissed her inner ankle, watching her face as he did. He wanted to savor this time with her.

Her chest rose and fell erratically as he slowly kissed a path up her legs, closer and closer to his end target.

By the time he reached her inner thigh, her breathing was out of control, her dark eyes dilated as she watched him hungrily. When he finally buried his face against her heat, she speared her fingers through his hair, holding on tight.

He liked the bite of pain from her nails as she writhed against him in complete abandonment. He loved that about her, that during sex, she didn't hold back anything. No insecurities, nothing, she just gave as good as she took.

He groaned against her slick folds, reveling in how wet she already was—all for him.

"Not gonna take me long," she managed to whisper.

Good. As he continued teasing her clit with his tongue, he slid two fingers inside her.

She arched off the desk as he thrust forward, curling his fingers back. That was what set her off. As she jerked against him, her inner walls clenched around his thrusting fingers and he didn't ease up on her clit. He continued teasing and tasting until she squeezed his head.

"Enough," she gasped out, falling limp against the desk for a moment.

He pushed up, looking down at her splayed out, her dress shoved up to her waist, her sex glistening from his mouth and her own release. She was sexy.

Suddenly she shoved up from the desk, the spaghetti straps on her dress falling loosely around her shoulders.

He tugged them all the way down because he wanted to see more of her, *all* of her. Her dress pooled around her waist and he immediately tugged her bandeau bra down before sucking one nipple into his mouth.

She shuddered, moaning at his teasing even as she started working the button on his jeans. She had him freed in moments, her long, delicate artist's fingers clenching around his hard length. He rolled his hips forward into her strokes, loving the way she gripped him tight.

"Move back," she whispered as she scooted to the edge of the desk. For a brief moment, disappointment flared inside him when she released him, but then she slid off the edge and turned over, bending over the desk.

Oh, hell yes.

With her round ass up in the air, her watching him over her shoulder, this was his fantasy come to life. Autumn was his fantasy. Everything about her called to him on the most primal level.

He ran his palm over her soft ass cheek as he guided himself to her slick entrance on a groan. She was so damn tight, and he'd missed her for far too long.

As he slowly thrust forward, savoring every second of this, her inner walls clenched around him tight.

She sucked in a breath and let her head tilt forward, her long dark hair falling down her back like a waterfall as he began thrusting. But he needed to touch more of her, so he reached around her body, cupping her breasts. He teased one of her nipples, rolling it between his thumb and forefinger, and pushed deep inside her.

"Lincoln," she moaned, pushing her ass back against him, meeting him stroke for stroke.

Each time he teased her nipple, he felt her inner walls contract harder around him. She could come again, he could feel it.

He was already so damn close to climaxing he didn't think he'd be able to last, not after fantasizing about her for the last nine weeks. No, he had Autumn in his arms and underneath him again and he wasn't letting her go.

"Faster," she demanded suddenly, her voice tight with need.

He could definitely oblige. He thrust harder and dropped his hand from her breast to her clit, hoping to wring another orgasm from her as he pumped inside her.

The faster he thrust, the more she trembled.

He lost all sense of time as his climax built inside him, his balls pulling up tight with a raw need.

When she cried out his name, her back bowing for one long moment as her orgasm hit, he finally let go.

As she came, he emptied himself inside her, reveling in the fact that he was completely bare. The most primitive part of his brain took over and he felt as if he were marking her. Every second of this was pure heaven and he wanted to claim her, forever.

Though he hated to separate from her, he eventually pulled out of her, wincing slightly as cool air rushed over his now half-hard length. They needed to clean up, but he just wanted to hold her.

"This was an incredible way to end the night," she said with a soft laugh as she turned around, completely rumpled and perfectly sexy.

Every territorial instinct lit up. *Mine.*

In response, he cupped her cheek and kissed her, softly this time, gently stroking his tongue against hers, trying to tell her without words how much she meant to him.

She linked her fingers together behind his neck, holding tight as she pressed her breasts to his chest. In that moment, he wished he'd had the mental capacity to remember to take his damn shirt off earlier, but all he'd been focused on was getting inside her.

"You want to stay over at my place tonight?" she whispered as she pulled back.

Surprised by the offer, he nodded. No way in hell would he ever say no to her.

And something told him that this was the beginning of something real between them. He hadn't been kidding, they'd done things backward with her getting pregnant so soon, but he didn't care. Normal was overrated anyway.

He wanted her in his life forever.

CHAPTER TWENTY-SEVEN

As Autumn knocked on Lincoln's front door, ready for their date, her phone rang. When she saw her mechanic's phone number, she immediately answered just as Lincoln opened the door.

She mouthed the word sorry as she answered.

"Hey, Enzo" she said.

"Hey, Autumn," Enzo said. "Sorry for calling so late, but I wanted to let you know that your tire is in. You can pick it up anytime you want this week as long as it's before five."

"Thanks. I'll stop by tomorrow after school." She followed Lincoln into his kitchen, inhaling whatever those delicious scents were—and staring at his fine ass as he moved.

"Sounds good. Listen, I looked at your tire again and found a bullet inside the rubber. I missed it originally because of the way it was lodged."

"Oh wow. So it was a bullet." That... was disturbing.

Lincoln shot her a look over his shoulder from the stove, but didn't say anything.

"Yeah, and I know you said you were on Industrial Road, but I still don't like it. That's dangerous shit right there."

"Did you save it?"

"Yeah. And I'm going to call the sheriff's department about it. I think Lincoln needs to know."

"I can tell Lincoln myself—I'm actually with him right now." She sat on the barstool at his island top. "But he'll probably want to see the bullet." She had no idea what kinds of testing the sheriff's department could do, but hopefully something.

Lincoln gave her a questioning look but didn't interrupt.

"Oh, I'll be dropping it off for sure."

After she'd wrapped up her conversation with Enzo, she quickly relayed what had happened to Lincoln, who had gone incredibly still as she told him everything.

"Did this happen the same day you had that confrontation with Mark Cadman?"

She paused, then nodded. "Yeah, but I seriously doubt it was him. I mean… I guess it could have been, but that seems like an extreme reaction."

"Cadman's an asshole." Lincoln's expression had gone dark now.

"Let's not talk about him," she said as she eyed the stove top. "Why don't you tell me what you're cooking?"

"We're going to talk about him later. I've already had one of my deputies bring him in for what he did at the school. He claimed he was just trying to talk to you, but he's been officially trespassed against the school. He's not allowed to be there anymore. Just so you know."

"Yeah, Sheila told me. And Mark's mom came in with their son. Mark Jr. was so embarrassed by what his dad did. Turns out he's struggling with his parents' divorce, mainly because he seems to hate his dad. He doesn't want to play football anymore and thought that if he failed my class, it would be an easy way to get benched instead of just quitting the team and pissing his dad off."

Lincoln shook his head as he headed back to the stove top. "That sounds like teenage logic for you."

She nodded. "It definitely does. So I'm letting him make up all of his work. And it looks like he's going to be quitting the team for his final year. I guess he only ever played for his dad and has no interest in it at all."

Lincoln shook his head, his jaw still tight. "Families can be complicated."

She snorted. "No kidding." She slid off the stool, not wanting any distance between them now. She leaned against the countertop next to him and inhaled in appreciation. "My mouth is literally watering right now."

He grinned. "This is one of the easiest things to make but it's always a winner, at least for me and my brothers. It's a simple rigatoni pasta with vodka cream sauce, shrimp, and I added a few vegetables like spinach because you can't taste it, but you're still getting all the nutrients."

"Not a vegetable man, are we?"

He lifted a broad shoulder. "I prefer meat and potatoes, but I still try to be healthy."

"I'm fish and veggies all the way." He'd asked her what she liked and she'd told him seafood and pasta, so it was clear that he'd made this with her in mind. So sweet. "Though I also eat anything Italian and with pasta, as you know."

He gave her another one of his panty-melting smiles and she had to remind herself to breathe. "I didn't get a chance to tell you that you look stunning tonight." Leaning over, he brushed his mouth against hers and a rush of pleasure speared through her.

"Thanks," she murmured. She'd worn slim-fitting jeans that rolled up at her ankles, gold kitten heels, and a bright red strappy top with lots of gold bangles and chandelier-style earrings. Her pants were already starting to pull just a bit at her waist and she knew that in roughly three weeks, she'd likely "pop" according to everything she'd read, so she was taking advantage and wearing her pants while she still could. "You look pretty good yourself."

"Thanks."

"So how was work today?" she asked.

"Very low-key thankfully. Just a lot of stupid calls."

"Stupid?"

"Yeah, and they always come in batches. One call was because someone was mad their neighbor was watching them out of their kitchen window. I don't know what they wanted us to do. And it turned out they weren't even watching their neighbor, they were simply washing the dishes and their window happens to face their neighbor's yard. Someone else called because their cable went out. That's pretty normal though."

She blinked. "That's normal?"

"Oh yeah, we get calls like that all the time. If the internet or satellite or cable go out in the area, we can count on at least half a dozen calls related to it. Apparently some people think we fix stuff like that." His tone was dry. "We also got a call out on Industrial Road where someone swears they saw a UFO."

"It would never occur to me to call the cops because my internet went out."

"I can't tell you how happy that makes me," he said on a laugh as he stirred the simmering sauce.

"You want me to put a salad together or anything?"

"It's all ready. It's in a covered container in the fridge if you want to grab it."

"This is a pretty nice date so far." She pulled out the oversized red container, served the salad into the two white bowls he'd already laid out on the island. He'd also already set out drinks for them, as well as lit a couple candles. The atmosphere was inviting and it meant a lot that he'd gone to this trouble for her. Tonight was... more than nice. She loved being here with Lincoln, seeing what things could be like between them. While she didn't want to get ahead of herself, things felt so right and she was almost afraid to enjoy it.

"I'm more than just a pretty face." Humor laced his words.

"You definitely are. So I know this is kind of a stupid thing to ask, but I also want open communication..."

He turned the stovetop off and moved the pan as he turned to look at her. "You can ask anything."

"I know this is officially a date for us, and since we're having a baby together this feels dumb to say but... Are you dating anyone else?" She was ninety-nine-point-nine percent sure the answer was no but she needed to hear him say it. Some deep-seated part of her absolutely needed to know that she was the only woman in his life right now. That she wasn't going to get a surprise later down the road and be blindsided.

He blinked at her, clearly stunned. "You think I'd be dating someone else?"

"Honestly no. But maybe I just need to hear that you're not." Oh God, she sounded so damn needy, but whatever.

He covered the distance between them, his big hands settling onto her hips. "Even before that night nine weeks ago, I hadn't dated anyone in ages. I've had my eye on someone for a long time—a sexy neighbor who seemed to want nothing to do with me."

The band of tension around her chest eased as she wrapped her arms around him. She was glad she had the right to touch him now, that they were taking this next step. "Okay good. I guess I'll give up dating now too," she said lightly, clearly joking.

He narrowed his gaze slightly, though she saw that he was fighting a laugh. "Good."

"I really want to kiss you now, but I'm also starving and I'm pretty sure the baby is hungry too."

He groaned softly and stepped back. "If we start, I don't think we'll stop. So sit and I'll serve you."

"I could get used to this you know," she said as she sat at the island while he scooped food onto their plates.

"Good, I want you to get used to this. I'm not changing, and I'm not going anywhere."

The little girl inside her who had always known there were decent men out there, the kind who wouldn't treat her the same way her mom had been treated, desperately wanted to believe his words. But it was hard to change old habits, old thought processes. Although he'd shown her who he was in everything he did, and she believed his actions as well as his words. She just needed to get her head on straight, to make sure her head and heart lined up with each other—because her heart wanted everything Lincoln had to offer.

"That was incredible. Your mom gets five stars for teaching you guys to cook," Autumn said after they'd finished dinner.

Lincoln grinned as he leaned back in his chair. He'd polished off all of his food and she'd managed to eat half of hers. She might not be getting full-on morning sickness, but she couldn't eat too much or she got nauseous. It was like this weird, delicate balance lately, making sure she ate enough to be satisfied but not too much that the baby revolted.

"She liked you, by the way," he said.

"Yeah?"

"Oh yeah. She thinks you're sweet and said I better not screw this up."

She laughed and took a sip of her drink. "She seems like the right type of mom for boys... Speaking of, do you care what we have? We haven't even talked about that." They'd vaguely discussed potential childcare options, but she wasn't even through the first trimester so they'd decided to hold off on any real decisions yet. Which was fine with her, she didn't need the extra stress.

"Nope." The answer was immediate, making her smile.

"I don't care either. Healthy is all that matters."

As he started to respond, his police radio went off.

She winced even as he groaned. "I'm on call tonight," he muttered as he stood and went to grab it.

He'd warned her that this might happen, but she'd been hoping that he wouldn't get any calls.

She sat back as he talked into his radio and by the time he was done, she knew that he was going to be leaving. She shoved down her disappointment because she understood that this was his job. And if she was going to be with him, she had to accept all of him. Starting now. It didn't squash her worry, however. She had a feeling that she'd always worry when he left.

"I'm so sorry," he said as he set his radio on the countertop. "Will you stay until I get back? This shouldn't take too long."

"Of course. If you don't mind, I'll grab Shadow and then come back here and at least clean up for you. I'm assuming you have some kind of dessert or something?" she asked hopefully. There'd been a white box in the fridge with a sticker from Sweet Spot on it.

He grinned at her, and butterflies took flight in her stomach. "I might happen to have your favorite chocolate cake in the fridge."

"You know the way to my heart. It's definitely through my stomach." She grabbed the front of his shirt and tugged him down to her. Worry rose sharp inside her, threatening to cut away at her, but she ignored it. Yes, she might worry about him, but that was okay.

He brushed his lips over hers, then groaned as he pulled back. "I really do have to run. But I've got my phone on me."

"Don't worry about me. I'm going to bring Shadow over after you leave and this place will be all cleaned up by the time you get back. Maybe you'll get lucky tonight too."

"I don't like the thought of you cleaning up the kitchen. This was supposed to be a date."

She shrugged. "I'm not leaving a mess for you. I'd be a pretty bad date if I did."

He looked like he still didn't like the idea, but kissed her again and then grabbed his keys, duty belt and a jacket that said sheriff on it. Apparently he was going to be heading out in mostly plainclothes. Hopefully that meant he wouldn't be long.

Once Lincoln left, she headed to the front door, her own keys in hand. She'd left Shadow at home because she'd forgotten to ask Lincoln about bringing her, but she didn't like leaving her alone for too long. Even during the week she had a service that came by and walked her during the day.

As she made her way across the front yard toward her house, she shivered at how dark it was. The street light must be out, and even with her front porch light on, everything felt darker than normal.

Picking up her pace, a tingling at the back of her neck made her turn around. As she did, pain exploded in the back of her skull and she fell forward onto her knees and hands.

Blinking, she tried to crawl forward, her fingers digging into the grass. *What the hell—*

Another blast of pain exploded, then darkness overtook her.

CHAPTER TWENTY-EIGHT

Pain fractured through Autumn's skull as she struggled toward consciousness. Her eyelids felt as if they had weights on them as she tried to force them open. Oh God, her head. A steady pulse of agony beat against her skull.

As she opened her eyes, a blue and gray rug came into view. Dark wood floors. A dresser. Where the hell was she?

"Took you long enough to wake up," a male voice said calmly.

She blinked, trying to open her eyes despite the pain. She was in a bedroom. It smelled like Lincoln but the man peering down at her with a sick grin on his face was definitely not Lincoln.

Fear punched through her when she recognized Tom Coventry.

Rand's father?

She wanted to ask him what the hell he was doing, but it was pretty clear what he'd done and why he was here. He was here to kill her. He'd somehow knocked her out and now she was... She tugged on her hands, which were bound behind her back. She was tied up in Lincoln's bedroom! *Oh God, the baby.*

Adrenaline punched through her, shoving away some of the cobwebs in her fuzzy mind. "How'd you find me?"

The question came out more as a raspy whisper. She winced at the mere sound of her own voice, the pain in her head making it hard to think, let alone speak. There was a dull throb of blood rushing in her ears as she struggled to sit up against the dresser. Her hip hurt. He hadn't even bothered to dump her on the bed; he must've just tossed her onto the hard floor.

"By being patient and having a lot of money," he spat at her as he crouched down, a wicked-looking blade in his hand.

It took everything in her not to stare at the knife. She knew if she did, the fear would overtake her and she would start panicking. If she was going to get out of this alive—and she had no idea how that was possible—she had to be smart. She had to survive.

Fear was a staccato beat in her chest, but she took a steady breath. "If you kill me, the marshals will know it was you." If he'd found her, he obviously knew she was in WITSEC.

"Oh, I'm going to kill you, but it won't be an easy death. I'm going to kill your boyfriend too. And the marshals won't be able to do shit about it."

She glared up at him, fighting past her fear and the nausea shoving at her throat. "I wouldn't be so sure about that."

He brandished the knife inches away from her face. "You took everything from me," he snarled. "And I'm going to take everything from you." He shoved up then, his boots pounding against the floor as he stomped away from her. "My wife left me! My son was stuck in jail for ten years! And I lost my chance at making it to the Senate. All because you couldn't mind your own business."

She knew that no matter what she said, it wouldn't matter. Still... "I didn't kill that girl."

"She was a nobody," he snapped. "Absolutely worthless. A stupid drug addict who would have died anyway."

That was the way the defense had tried to spin it, putting the victim on trial. But they'd never been able to prove that she was actually an addict, not that it should have mattered anyway. Maybe it was true, or maybe Tom Coventry had started to believe his own narrative.

"You and I are going to have a little fun before I kill you. Your carved-up body is going to be the first thing your pathetic boyfriend sees when he walks in the door." An evil gleam glinted in his eyes as he stalked toward her and crouched down again.

As he did, she heard the front door open downstairs.

Panic a live wire inside her, she opened her mouth to scream but he slapped his hand over it. She bit down on one of his fingers. Teeth bared, he winced but didn't cry out as he yanked her to her feet and twisted her around, pulling her against him and cutting off her breathing with his forearm over her throat.

Lincoln! she silently cried out.

She tried to struggle against him, but he held his knife right to her abdomen as he choked her. She froze on instinct, not wanting him to stab her in the stomach. But spots swam before her eyes as she tried to drag in a breath. *Ohgodohgodohgod!*

CHAPTER TWENTY-NINE

Lincoln couldn't believe he'd left a date with Autumn for such a dumbass call. Originally the operator had told him it was a domestic incident, something he would never pass off to anyone else.

But it turned out it hadn't been domestic at all, but a very amorous couple who'd simply been loud. Their neighbors had called the cops, thinking the husband was hurting the wife. Nope, the exact opposite. They'd been confused and then embarrassed when he'd shown up. But at least no one had been hurt, and he hoped that he and Autumn got to the "dessert" part of the evening soon.

Desperate to see her, he took off his duty belt and jacket as he entered the kitchen. Frowning, he looked at the dirty plates and the food still uncovered. This...felt wrong. No way would Autumn have left his place like this. And her phone was still on the countertop, a little green light blinking. He glanced at it and saw she had an unread text from him.

In that moment, instinct kicked in—and he knew he wasn't alone in the house.

Something was wrong.

There was a soft squeaking sound and a slight shuffle coming from upstairs. Autumn had told him that she was going to get Shadow, but her dog wasn't here either. He didn't like any of this.

Withdrawing his weapon, he moved to his radio and turned it on, hoping the noise would cover his movements. Then he turned the dishwasher on even though there was nothing in it. It started with a whoosh. The extra noise should hopefully give the appearance of him being in the kitchen as he silently hunted down whoever was in his damn house.

He silently prayed that Autumn had made it home, that whatever was going on didn't involve her. But the dread spreading through his veins told him otherwise.

On silent feet, he eased up his stairs, his weapon in front of him as he eyed the landing above him. Through the railing, he could see into one of his guest rooms and see the door open to his own bedroom. The light was on, and not because of him. He turned off the light of any room he left—it had been drilled into him as a kid.

Maybe... Autumn was waiting for him in his bed? No, she hadn't called out or anything. Fear sank its claws into his spine, gripping tight.

He skipped over the fifth stair because it squeaked and tried to steady his breathing as he reached the top. Before he made it to the landing, he texted the deputy on duty, telling him he needed backup.

Hopefully this was all a mistake and Autumn was simply naked and in his bed, but his gut was telling him something else was going on here.

When he heard a shuffling and then what sounded like a cry, he moved quickly to the landing, blood rushing in his ears.

Crouching low, he had his weapon out as he swept into his room.

The sight that greeted him froze the blood in his veins.

An older man—Tom Coventry, from the image he'd found of the guy when he'd looked him up online—had a knife pressed to Autumn's neck as he used her as a shield.

"Drop your weapon now," he snarled, only his training preventing him from pulling the trigger.

"You're going to drop *your* weapon." Coventry's hand shook but he didn't move, didn't give Lincoln the opening he needed to end him.

"You haven't hurt her yet." Or he prayed he hadn't. Lincoln kept his gaze off Autumn, because he knew that if he looked at her face, made eye contact, it would do more than distract him. He had to stay as detached as possible, had to save her and their baby. That meant listening to all his training when all he wanted to do was attack this bastard. "Just put your weapon down and you can still recover from this. You can still walk away."

"You're going to put down your gun, and then you and I are going to talk," the man said, his hand trembling again slightly. When he did, he nicked her, blood trickling down her neck.

Lincoln's saw red in that moment, barely controlled himself. The only thing holding him back was that his actions could get her hurt. "Listen to me—"

"Behind you!" she suddenly screamed.

Moving on instinct, he spun, and tackled a hard male body.

A man snarled and a fist slammed against his back as Lincoln tackled the guy, flying through the doorway and crashing into the banister railing.

It gave way under the impact and they flew through the air. Autumn screamed and the man let out a short cry as they slammed against the stairs with a sickening crunch.

CHAPTER THIRTY

All the air left Autumn's lungs as Lincoln dropped out of sight. In the same instance, rage like she'd never known took over. She screamed and kicked backward as hard as she could. She had to get to Lincoln, he had to be okay!

Her heel connected with something. Behind her, Tom Coventry howled in pain as she lunged forward. He should have bound her legs too.

With her hands tied, she couldn't fight him, but she could run. She had to get to Lincoln, get help.

She sprinted through the doorway, slamming her shoulder against the frame as she ran. She bit back a cry of pain as she skidded on the hallway floor, her momentum almost too much. Instead of tumbling over the edge of the banister, she made a sharp right and stumbled toward the top of the stairs.

"You stupid bitch!" he shouted behind her.

She swore she could feel him breathing down her neck as she lurched forward, tripping on the hallway runner and slamming into the banister railing at the top of the stairs.

Her eyes widened when she saw Lincoln on top of Rand Coventry's unmoving body. Lincoln was on his knees, his hand clutching the bottom of the stair railing as he pulled himself up. He was alive!

He looked up at her—and his expression froze. "Duck!" Lincoln's voice boomed through the air.

She didn't even think, just did as he said and dove for the floor, her head hitting the wood as a loud bang rent the air.

Then another.

Her whole body jerked at the blast of gunfire. She rolled onto her back, her arms straining under the ropes. Tom Coventry staggered forward, eyes wide, knife raised into the air as he fell toward her. Blood poured out of two chest wounds.

She scrambled out of the way, rolling as he crashed to the floor right next to her, impaling his knife into it with a thud.

"Autumn!"

She heard thumps on the stairs and then Lincoln was there, untying her hands and turning her over. Heart pounding, she threw her arms around him as he lifted her into his arms. "Lincoln," she sobbed, the sound ripping out of her. She could have lost him, almost did. She could have died herself. Oh, God. This was all too much.

"It's over, they can't hurt you," he murmured soothingly as he hurried down the stairs with her.

"How bad are you hurt?" He'd fallen off the damn landing! He was limping as he struggled down the stairs. She didn't even know how he was walking.

She was vaguely aware of Rand Coventry's prone body as they passed him on the stairs—his neck was twisted at an unnatural angle. There was no need to even check his pulse. He was dead. And she was glad.

"I'm a little banged up. How are you? Did he hurt you?" He hurried down the hallway just as his front door flew open.

Two deputies stormed in, weapons up. They immediately dropped their weapons when they saw her and Lincoln.

"Let me get her outside," Lincoln snapped. "Secure the scene now." The two men nodded and hurried past them.

He was walking in jerky motions as he stumbled through the door, and she realized that he might be more hurt than he'd said.

"Put me down," she insisted as they reached the front porch. Her entire body felt numb as she tried to digest what had just happened—she wasn't sure that she ever would.

He did and then sagged against one of the columns, the muscles in his forearm flexing with the movement.

"Oh, Lincoln." She took him in, saw he had a split lip, his forearm had been sliced up and he had a bruise forming on the side of his cheek. He was holding on to his side and breathing seemed to be a struggle. "Are your ribs bothering you?" If she focused on him, she wouldn't focus on the fact that there were two dead people in his house—two people who had come to kill her. Likely torture her.

"I'm fine," he murmured, but his face was pale and when she motioned for him to sit down, he didn't argue—which told her how bad he must feel.

Blessed sirens wailed in the distance as she collapsed next to him on the little set of stairs. Help would be here soon. The sound exacerbated the growing ache in her skull, but she tried to ignore it.

She scooted closer to him, cold snaking through her. She needed to get warm. "If you hadn't come home, he would've killed me." Her voice shook as she got the words out. She should save this for later, but she couldn't stop talking as she grabbed his hand in hers, squeezed tight. "I didn't even know his son was there. They... They would've done more than just kill me." She knew that without a shadow of a doubt now. Clearly they'd had some sort of plan—they'd been smart enough to do something with his dental records. Now she understood why the DNA test had been corrupted—she guessed it was mixed with the body of whoever had actually been in that crash. Because it hadn't been Rand Coventry. They must have been waiting to get her alone and jumped at the chance. Maybe Rand had been backup or something for when Lincoln arrived.

Lincoln wrapped his arm around her shoulder even as he waved off one of his deputies and ordered them to give him and Autumn space. He winced as he pulled her close. "That bastard will never hurt you again. Neither of them will."

The tears came then, fully flowing as the ambulance screeched up to the front of his house. In that moment, her feelings for Lincoln were crystal clear. She'd been so damn afraid of losing him to violence, of losing him on the job, but her own past had come back to haunt her and had almost killed them both. Ripped them apart when they'd only just found their way to each other. "I love you."

His whole body jerked as he looked at her, his eyes widening. Then he smiled, wincing and cradling his ribs again. "I love you too. And you're moving in with me."

"Sir—"

He held up a hand as an EMT she vaguely recognized hurried toward them. "Hold on," he said as he turned to her. "We love each other, we're having a baby together, and you're moving in."

"I love you, Lincoln, but you're going to the hospital right now." Groaning, she got to her feet and turned to the woman. "I think he's got a couple broken ribs. He fell off the top of the stairs. He needs to be taken to the hospital immediately."

The woman nodded as her partner hurried up with a stretcher. "You're coming with us too. Your eyes are too dilated."

"Yeah, I might have a concussion," she muttered. Her head was throbbing and the adrenaline was starting to fade, but they were alive.

And Lincoln loved her back. She was never letting him go, never letting fear rule her life again.

CHAPTER THIRTY-ONE

Three days later

Autumn stepped outside onto her half-built back deck, watching Easton, Lucas and two of their friends hard at work.

Lincoln stepped up beside her, unable to do any work because of his cracked ribs. Two to be exact. He shouldn't even be up right now. He'd been resting in her living room when she'd left him.

"Pretty sure you just hurt yourself to get out of all this work," Easton grumbled good-naturedly as he hammered a nail into one of the beams.

Autumn snorted. "You better be nice to your brother or I'm not going to order you any pizza or beer."

Easton lifted up a hand in mock surrender. "I'm kidding! In fact, drag him inside and make him sit down. He needs to be resting anyway." Easton shot Lincoln an annoyed look.

"He's right," Lucas said without looking up. "Make sure he gets his ass back in the chair, Autumn. We've got this."

"I'm right here," Lincoln muttered.

"Yeah, but you heard the doctor's orders, come on." She gently guided him through her kitchen and led him to her brightly lit living room and plunked him down in

251

her favorite chair. Shadow nestled right up next to his feet and curled up beside her new favorite person.

Lincoln looked like a grumpy bear as he sat there. "This is ridiculous. I'm fine. I could go out there and help them right now."

She made an incredulous sound. "Oh yeah, you're super fine. The doctor was lying to you for shits and giggles."

His mouth twitched as he looked up at her. "You're very bossy."

"Don't you forget it," she said as she leaned down and brushed her lips gently over his. She couldn't believe she'd almost lost him—might have died herself. The US Marshals were rightfully upset about what happened and had taken extra steps to ensure she wasn't in any more danger.

It didn't look as if she was—the Coventrys were the only two people who had wanted her dead. Rand's mother had remarried and moved on with her life years ago, apparently. She hadn't spoken to either of them in a solid four years. It turned out that they'd paid off someone at the prison to alter the dental records because they'd known those would be checked first. That person who'd helped them? Now dead.

The reason the DNA results had been corrupted was because their DNA had been planted with two dead, burned bodies. She had no idea where the dead bodies had come from, but she was sure the marshals would figure all that out eventually. It was just dumb luck that their DNA had even been picked up for the first test. The men who'd helped Tom Coventry bust his son and that other guy out had never planned for the DNA to hold up under scrutiny—they'd just wanted to get the prisoners free and out of the country. Tom had been planning to bust his son out of jail for a while—he'd just been working on getting the right help to do it.

Tom Coventry had worked for some dangerous drug runners, helping them to hide their money—and he'd asked for a favor. He'd wanted his son out of jail, but hadn't had the man or firepower to do it. Since that had aligned with rescuing someone related to one of the drug runners, they'd worked it so that both men would be on the same transport at the same time. They'd paid off people for that too. She was just glad that no one else was after her anymore.

He groaned. "I hate not being able to touch you."

"You can still touch me, just not... You know." She cupped his face, needing to touch *him*, to remind herself that he was okay. "Sit tight, I'm going to get you something to drink." As she hurried to the kitchen, she couldn't help but be thankful—for like the hundredth time—that they were both okay.

She'd been having nightmares, imagining that Rand and his father had succeeded and killed both of them. That when Lincoln and that bastard had tumbled over the railing, Lincoln had died. She shuddered at the thought.

Over the last few nights, she'd woken up drenched in sweat, but Lincoln had been right next to her. So had Shadow.

She knew it would get better, and she was going to start going back to therapy again. She hadn't gone in years, but after what had happened, she knew she had to now. It didn't matter that she was no longer under threat, she needed to talk some things out.

The marshals had also used their resources and discovered that the bullet from her tire had been from Mark Cadman. Something that surprised her. He'd taken a shot at her—according to his confession—just to scare her. A lie. They'd also got a match to his boot print outside her window. He was just another angry man who had decided she was to blame for all his troubles.

Unfortunately for him, once they'd searched his house, they'd found a whole lot of bad shit on his computer—he was on some fringe websites and had been planning something even Erica wouldn't tell her about. All Autumn knew was that he'd be going away for a very long time. So she wasn't going to worry about him again. But she was grateful that the marshals had used their vast resources to help out the Verona Bay Sheriff's Department—and her. She knew it was out of guilt, but she didn't care. And the cherry on top of the insanity of the last couple months, the Feds had also found those jerk bank robbers. They'd gotten too greedy and it had gotten them caught. The world felt... right again. Hell, better than her version of normal.

She stepped back into the room with a glass of lemonade and some cookies she'd made.

His eyes lit up when he saw the cookies. "I just got off the phone with Erica," he said as she handed him the plate and set the drink on the table next to him.

"What did she say?" Autumn hadn't thought there could be any more news at this point.

"They discovered who gave your information to Coventry. A really skilled hacker they've been looking for."

She blinked as she sat across from him. "That's great. Is he... or she, a danger to me?"

"He, and nope. He hired someone to come to Verona Bay to make sure you were really here—and the hacker turned on the man he'd hired too, so he's going to be doing some time as well. Not that giving up the information matters for the hacker's prison sentence. They've got him for a whole lot of crimes. He's pissed off a lot of people over the years, from what Erica said. I don't think he'll last long in prison." He shrugged and took a bite of his cookie.

She sat back, feeling... settled.

"So are we going to move into your house or mine?" he bluntly asked.

Surprised, she stared at him. "You were serious about that?" He hadn't brought it up again.

"I was." His expression reflected his intent as he watched her carefully.

"Well, your brothers and their friends are building a nice new deck here. And my house has a little more room. We could rent out yours and stay here?"

He blinked in surprise. "You're not going to argue with me about this?"

"Should I?"

"No, I just thought I would get some pushback. Are you just saying this now because I'm injured? Is this a pity thing? Because I'll take it."

She shook her head, her mouth curving up slightly. He was a tad grouchy, which for some reason made her smile, seeing this side to him. It made him seem more human. "No. We're going to be in each other's bed every night, and I'll be having this kiddo in a few months. Plus, you know, we *love* each other. It doesn't make sense to live next door to each other in separate houses."

The grin he gave her was a balm to all of her senses. She could have lost him so easily, to such awful violence. And she knew violence could happen at any time so she wasn't going to worry about the what ifs anymore. They had each other right now, and she was going to hold on to him tight—as soon as his ribs healed, of course.

"You know I'm going to put a ring on your finger pretty soon." He spoke so matter-of-factly.

"Is that your idea of a proposal?"

"No. I'm just letting you know."

Her heart rate kicked up. The thought of being married to him was incredible, everything she'd never even known she wanted. But to be claimed by him? For the whole world to see? Her throat grew tight for a moment. "I'm not sure how to respond to that."

He simply grinned at her. "You don't need to. Just know that it's coming."

She wasn't sure if she was glad he'd told her or not. She just knew that if he asked her, she would say yes.

CHAPTER THIRTY-TWO

Christmas Day

Autumn sat in front of the Christmas tree in her—now, their—living room, waiting for Lincoln to hurry up with her hot chocolate.

He strode into the room with Shadow at his heels. Shadow had indeed become his actual shadow, following him around everywhere. It was the sweetest thing ever. He even took her to work sometimes. She'd become the unofficial mascot for the station. For a dog who had been abandoned and likely abused, she now had tons of people who loved and spoiled her.

"Thank you," she said as he handed her the steaming mug. Now that her bump was showing, he'd gone into a sort of wildly overprotective mode, refusing to let her do much of anything. It was ridiculous and adorable at the same time. And okay, being spoiled by the man she loved certainly wasn't a chore. She figured she'd better enjoy all of this now while she could, because in a few months, they were going to be running on no sleep. At least according to all of her mom friends.

"Can we open the presents now?" she asked, squirming in her seat on the floor. They'd be going over to his parents' in the afternoon, but this morning was just for them, and she was enjoying every second of it.

"You're like a kid," he said as he pulled out a small box and handed it to her, a mischievous grin on his face.

"This wrapping is so pretty." She ran her fingers over the dark crimson and gold. It was about the size of a couple books and since he knew her so well, she kinda figured it was the thriller collection she'd been eyeing at the local bookstore earlier in the week. She loved her e-reader, but there were some books she liked to keep on her shelf in print.

"You have to open one too," she said as she leaned over and snagged a present with dog-themed wrapping paper. The dog looked just like Shadow, so she'd grabbed it.

"I will, but you go first." He was watching her intently as he sat across from her, sipping on his own drink—coffee, something she still desperately missed.

"Okay." She ripped into it like a savage, not bothering to save the paper because yes, she felt like a kid at the moment. So many Christmases she'd spent alone or with friends, but she'd always felt like an outsider. As if no one would actually miss her if she wasn't there.

Right now, she felt as if her heart was near to bursting. She was spending Christmas Day with the man she loved, the father of her child, in their house as they got ready for their future. When she opened the brown box, she saw another, much smaller ring-sized box in the center of a bunch of tissue paper. And she recognized the logo of a local jeweler.

Her heart kicked against her ribs as she stared at it, not the baby this time. Just a wild, beating anticipation.

She thought she knew what this was. She hoped it was, anyway.

"Open it," he softly ordered.

Apparently she waited too long, because he plucked it from her and opened the box himself, holding it out as he crouched in front of her.

"You sweet, wonderful woman, will you marry me?"

"Yes." She didn't have to think, didn't have to second-guess herself. No matter how many times he asked, she would say yes every time.

He shoved out a breath of what definitely sounded like relief—though how he could have doubted her answer by now was beyond her. He slid the ring onto her finger and as she stared down at it, tears spilled over. She'd never thought she would have a family of her own, and never with someone as wonderful as Lincoln.

"It's beautiful," she whispered as she leaned forward, kissing him.

"You're beautiful," he said against her mouth.

The baby kicked, startling her. She grabbed his hand and held it to her stomach. The little peanut kicked again, making both of them smile.

"Maybe when you launch your new website," he said, "you can operate as Autumn Jordan."

Her throat grew thick with more tears and she nodded, unable to find any words in that moment. She wanted to be a Jordan more than anything. Once all the dust had cleared a few months ago, and she'd officially been able to go back to her life "before", she'd decided to remain Autumn Perez. But she'd been allowed to contact old friends as well, including Hector, who was planning to visit her in the new year. She was also getting back into photography and had planned to set up a small studio.

To start this new chapter of her life with the same last name as the man she loved? Oh yeah. "Nothing would make me happier," she finally managed to get out.

She finally had her life back, she could do what she loved once again with no worries that her art would bring killers to her doorstep. She was free to live her life with the man she loved and the family they were creating.

As incredible as it seemed, all her dreams were becoming reality.

Thank you for reading Deadly Past. If you'd like to stay in touch with Katie and be the first to learn about new releases, sign up for her newsletter at

https://katiereus.com

ACKNOWLEDGMENTS

As always I owe a huge thanks to Kaylea Cross, the best critique partner a writer could ask for! I'm also grateful to my editor, Kelli Collins, to Jaycee for another amazing cover, to Sarah for proofreading, to Amy for formatting, and of course to my fabulous readers! Thank every single one of you. Writing a book is just the first step. Getting it in shape to publish is the next one and I'm grateful to have such a great team to help me do that.

COMPLETE BOOKLIST

Ancients Rising Series
Ancient Protector
Ancient Enemy
Ancient Enforcer

Darkness Series
Darkness Awakened
Taste of Darkness
Beyond the Darkness
Hunted by Darkness
Into the Darkness
Saved by Darkness
Guardian of Darkness
Sentinel of Darkness
A Very Dragon Christmas
Darkness Rising

Deadly Ops Series
Targeted
Bound to Danger
Chasing Danger (novella)
Shattered Duty
Edge of Danger
A Covert Affair

Endgame Trilogy
Bishop's Knight
Bishop's Queen
Bishop's Endgame

MacArthur Family Series
Falling for Irish
Unintended Target
Saving Sienna

Moon Shifter Series
Alpha Instinct
Lover's Instinct
Primal Possession
Mating Instinct
His Untamed Desire
Avenger's Heat
Hunter Reborn
Protective Instinct
Dark Protector
A Mate for Christmas

O'Connor Family Series
Merry Christmas, Baby
Tease Me, Baby
It's Me Again, Baby
Mistletoe Me, Baby

Red Stone Security Series®
No One to Trust
Danger Next Door
Fatal Deception
Miami, Mistletoe & Murder
His to Protect
Breaking Her Rules
Protecting His Witness
Sinful Seduction
Under His Protection
Deadly Fallout
Sworn to Protect
Secret Obsession
Love Thy Enemy
Dangerous Protector
Lethal Game

Redemption Harbor Series®
Resurrection
Savage Rising
Dangerous Witness
Innocent Target
Hunting Danger
Covert Games
Chasing Vengeance

Sin City Series (the Serafina)
First Surrender
Sensual Surrender
Sweetest Surrender
Dangerous Surrender

Verona Bay
Dark Memento
Deadly Past

Linked books
Retribution
Tempting Danger

Non-series Romantic Suspense
Running From the Past
Dangerous Secrets
Killer Secrets
Deadly Obsession
Danger in Paradise
His Secret Past

Paranormal Romance
Destined Mate
Protector's Mate
A Jaguar's Kiss
Tempting the Jaguar
Enemy Mine
Heart of the Jaguar

ABOUT THE AUTHOR

Katie Reus is the *New York Times* and *USA Today* bestselling author of the Red Stone Security series, the Darkness series and the Deadly Ops series. She fell in love with romance at a young age thanks to books she pilfered from her mom's stash. Years later she loves reading romance almost as much as she loves writing it.

However, she didn't always know she wanted to be a writer. After changing majors many times, she finally graduated summa cum laude with a degree in psychology. Not long after that she discovered a new love. Writing. She now spends her days writing dark paranormal romance and sexy romantic suspense. For more information on Katie please visit her website: https://katiereus.com

Made in the USA
Coppell, TX
10 November 2020